let us
DREAM

Alyssa Cole

Dear Tiffany,
Never stop
~~~~ &!
~~~~ ssr
Cole

LET US DREAM
Copyright Alyssa Cole © 2016

ACKNOWLEDGMENTS

Many thanks to Mala Bhattacharjee and Farah Ghuznavi for their help with the linguistic and cultural aspects of the story. Also, Colleen Katana, Derek Bishop, Krista Amigone, and my anthology mates for their invaluable feedback.

Applauding youths laughed with young prostitutes
And watched her perfect, half-clothed body sway;
Her voice was like the sound of blended flutes
Blown by black players upon a picnic day.
She sang and danced on gracefully and calm,
The light gauze hanging loose about her form;
To me she seemed a proudly-swaying palm
Grown lovelier for passing through a storm.
Upon her swarthy neck black shiny curls
Luxuriant fell; and tossing coins in praise,
The wine-flushed, bold-eyed boys, and even the girls,
Devoured her shape with eager, passionate gaze;
But looking at her falsely-smiling face,
I knew her self was not in that strange place.

Claude McKay, "The Harlem Dancer"

"They come with their laws and their codes to bind me fast; but I evade them ever, for I am only waiting for love to give myself up at last..."

Rabindranath Tagore

chapter one

October 1917
Harlem, New York

"Hold your ear down, 'less you wanna get burnt again." Nell's accent, cultivated in the rich soil of the Deep South, slipped through the racket of the hair salon on a Saturday afternoon. Her voice was warm and sweet, like a peach right off the tree, and Bertha closed her eyes at the feeling of home it stirred in her. It reminded her of that brief happy time where she'd awoken in the same bed every morning and helped her mama with the cleaning before heading off to school or dance lessons.

Strains of different conversations swirled through the Glossine-scented air of the salon: Negro boys getting sent off to fight in France, and maybe to die there too; the latest show put on by the Lafayette Players over at the theater; and, of course, the upcoming elections.

"My man barely wanted to let me come to the shop for a few hours. He ain't thinking about letting me near a ballot box," one woman said. Laughter circled around the shop, the tense kind that happened when a joke wasn't really a joke but you either laughed or despaired. Bertha didn't laugh; she kept clear of entanglements with men because she was now in a position to do so, and they still controlled most aspects of her life. Even she couldn't muster the fake joviality to laugh at what these women, who had a fraction of her autonomy, faced.

"You want that ear or no, Miss Hines?" Nell asked.

Bertha pulled her ear down flat with her index and middle fingers, remaining stock still as the heat of the metal comb warmed the oil on her scalp and the sensitive skin on the backs of her fingers. She stared down at the brown skirt peeking out from under the protective sheet Nell had draped over her before commencing to straighten Bertha's long, thick hair. She was wearing the dowdiest dress she owned; long, drab, high-collared. It was yet another costume, this one designed to cover up instead of reveal. Something told her the crowd at Colored Women's Voting League wouldn't go for the sequins, bangles, and silk that made up her usual nightly wardrobe.

"You learned from your mistake last time," Nell chuckled, placing the comb down on the metal warming plate and running a brush through Bertha's hair. "Still as a statue."

"You're the one who burned my neck last time, so I think you're the one who learned," Bertha reminded her.

"You had everyone in the Cashmere thinking I had a love bite."

She lifted her head the slightest bit to cut her eyes at Nell's reflection in the mirror.

Nell made a sound between a laugh and a snort of disbelief. "A love bite at the Cashmere is about as common as a spot on a leopard."

Nell was only teasing, but her words plucked at Bertha's already taut nerves. She straightened her spine to its usual rigid alignment and lifted her shoulders back. "There's nothing common about it when we're talking about *me*."

She used the tone that had gotten her through the last few years, the one that reminded people of exactly who she was. Of course, she had been exactly nobody when she first started using it, but people didn't want to have to think too hard, really—they believed what you presented them with.

Girl, people see what they want to see; they take the path of least resistance. We just got to lead them down the path that benefits us. Ain't nothing wrong with that, hear me?

Her father had been many things, but foolish wasn't one of them. Bertha gifted people with the idea that she was not to be treated lightly, and they responded accordingly. No one had thought a poor Black whore audacious enough to bend the truth in such a way, and she had benefited from it, plain and simple.

Nell paused in the intricate chignon she had begun creating and caught Bertha's gaze in the mirror. Her eyes were wide in her toffee-toned face, and her mouth hung slightly open as she realized that Bertha hadn't appreciated her jab.

"You know I don't mean nothing bad, Miss Hines."

"Nell, you heard anything from your cousin who applied at the hospital?" Sandra, a local washerwoman who was getting a conditioning treatment in the chair next to Bertha, interrupted, either out of rudeness or to head off any awkwardness. Bertha was glad, whatever the reason; she didn't want to embarrass Nell if she could help it.

Nell's fingers flexed against Bertha's scalp as she resumed her work, grabbing up long hanks of hair, twisting and pinning. "Yes, ma'am. She got the job. Got her a nice white uniform hanging in her closet. Used so much starch I don't know how she gonna bend over!"

"Well, good!" Sandra beamed, slapping her thigh beneath the sheet covering her clothes. "I didn't believe it when they said they was hiring Negro nurses now. My sister can come up from Charlotte and get a job here when she done with school."

Bertha thought of how she'd come to New York with hopes of a good, respectable job, too. How so many women, fleeing the restraints of the South, had. She thought of telling Sandra how a chunk of the White nurses had resigned, rather than work with Negro women. But Sandra was looking at her expectantly, so she smiled and nodded benevolently—she was a performer after all. Her daddy had once told her that pretending was a full-time job. Bertha had thought him full of it, but wasn't she her father's child now?

"Well, wouldn't that be something!" she said, flashing a grin at Sandra. "I bet she'll snap up a position in no time."

The door to the salon opened and the cool autumn air danced through the scent of flower-infused oil, miracle growth conditioner, and singed hair, carrying in the smell of roasted nuts from the vendor down the street. A young boy entered, straightening the lapel on his too-large suit.

"Anybody got numbers for Miss Queenie?" The expression on his still-round face was comically serious, a replica of the older number runners who posted up on corners and visited businesses throughout the day, taking people's money and leaving them with a bit of hope.

"Boy, get in here and stop letting out all the heat," one of the other hair dressers called out. "And give me my usual numbers, boxed."

She handed the boy some coins and he noted something on a slip of paper before stuffing it in his pocket.

"Oh, I had a dream last night. My mama told me to go to building seven-three-one. I'm gonna play that," another woman said. The crowd in the salon voiced their support of the idea.

"What about you, miss?" the boy asked. He had wide, innocent eyes—too innocent to be caught up in the numbers racket already. But Bertha knew all too well that age didn't mean anything once money was involved.

"Not for me," she said.

He nodded and jogged out the door, running off to pick up more bets and carry them back to the number hole.

"All done," Nell said, whipping off the protective sheet and dusting off the back of Bertha's dress. Bertha stood and examined her hair in the mirror for a minute. It was unremarkable, which was exactly what she wanted. She handed Nell her due, plus a good tip to make up for getting high and mighty with her. She liked the woman—and Nell hadn't been wrong.

"You sure look nice," Sandra said, eyeing the high-necked brown dress and matching jacket. "You goin' to church or somethin'?"

Bertha smiled. "Something." She took a look at the women crowded in the shop: hair dressers, laundresses, domestics. She was doing this for them. She pinned on her wide-brimmed brown hat, took one last look in the mirror, and then headed out onto the street.

It was Saturday afternoon, and if she hadn't known already, she would have as soon as she turned onto Lenox Ave. The traffic was bumper to bumper, and the line of trolleys, horses, and Model Ts made her glad she had decided to walk off her nervous excitement. The sidewalks were packed with people strolling, out showing off their autumn outfits as they walked slowly up and down the street. The clusters of people she navigated through grew and shrank as people drifted away from conversations with one group and into them with another.

She had no time to stop and talk, either with acquaintances or with strangers in the mood to chat, as she headed for the meeting. She went over her planned speech in her head.

We need the vote, and I have a plan, you see...

"Hey, Miss B!" She was pulled from her planning by a familiar voice—and the familiar scent of chicken and collard greens. The mix of tangy and savory aromas brought her back in time, to when mama would make dinner and the family would all eat together, back before her father discovered his surefire moneymaking venture and pulled her away from family and school and into his obsessive scheme.

Your mama's too dark, and she don't got good hair, like us...

"Hey, Mary." Bertha slowed but didn't stop, as she walked by the woman's bizarre portable stove tucked into a baby carriage. Well, there were two carriages now—Mary's business was expanding along with the rest of the neighborhood. "Still no chance I can lure you to my kitchen?"

Mary laughed. "The Cashmere too fancy for my simple cooking. Don't tell me you got folks in there eating chitlins in their fixy dresses!"

Bertha laughed. "One of these days, I'll change your mind, just to have that cornbread of yours in my kitchen every day," she said with a wink.

Mary looked down, bashful. "This corner ain't glamorous, but I like being my own boss woman. You know how that is."

"That I do, Mary. Good afternoon!"

Bertha walked away with renewed purpose. Women like Mary needed her to do this, too.

She arrived at the Colored Women's Voting League building, following the other women who entered without the slightest hesitation. She could tell from their clothes and their hats and the way their eyes were a little wary as they greeted her, even in her nice dress and make-up free face, that these were *good* women. Upstanding, pillars of the community, and all the things she wasn't.

Her stomach tightened but she pulled her shoulders back and lifted her chin.

You belong here just as much as them. Act like it.

She felt a sense of calm come over her as she eased into the role. She was a businesswoman, looking to protect her interests and those of the women who worked for her. These uptight suffragettes might look down on her, but they *would* hear her out.

A woman in a dress that looked like something fit for a funeral—to be buried in, that is—stepped onto the stage. She was light bright and tight-lipped, wearing no make-up, her hair brushed back into a simple bun. A preacher's daughter, if Bertha had ever seen one.

Bertha tried not to be critical of her, but she knew exactly what women like Delta Henderson thought of her. It was instinctive for her to size them up, look for weak spots, and, once discovered, to be ready to point them out the moment they dared talk down to her. Some men walked through dangerous territory with their guns cocked and ready, and Bertha did the same with her words. It had been the same on the road with her father, the same when she took over the Cashmere after her husband Arthur had died, and she wouldn't treat these women any differently, though she wished she could.

"Sisters, thank all of you so much for joining us at this important meeting," Delta said. She looked around, her eyes lit up with the kind of ridiculous hope that made Bertha roll her own. Hope wasn't going to get them the vote; it was time for action.

"One of the most important elections of our lifetimes is coming up one month from now," Delta said. "On that day, the men of New York state will be voting on whether we, their sistren, will finally be afforded the God-given right to vote."

Applause broke out in the room and Bertha joined in. The press of emotion in her throat at the possibility that lay before them annoyed her; it seemed hope was catching, like cooties. She cleared her throat and folded her hands in her lap, waiting for the applause to die down.

"Now, they had the same opportunity two years ago, and they did not make the correct decision."

Grumbling broke out amongst the women.

"I know. It's frustrating." Delta held out her hands and then lowered them, modulating the volume in the room like the conductor of a big band. Bertha grinned. Definitely a preacher's daughter.

"But we've made great strides since then. We've organized with the National Women's Voting League, the Women's Suffrage Union—too many wonderful groups to name—and the suffrage movement is more united than it has ever been."

Bertha was tempted to ask why they needed a separate organization—and a separate building—for Negro women if there was so much unity, but that would have been low. Besides, she knew why. They all knew why.

"But now we're in the last stretch of the race and we need to apply pressure," Delta continued, pressing the fist of one hand into the palm of the other. She looked out over the crowd with determination shining in her eyes. "We have to convince the men to vote yes. Speak to your husbands, brothers, cousins. Speak to your fellow congregants at church. To the brother lodges affiliated with your women's clubs. By now, we all know that we deserve the vote, but they need to know it too. They need to give it to us."

Raucous applause littered with "Amen!" broke out, but Bertha was no longer clapping. She was standing, one hand raised in the air. Delta Henderson's vibrant gaze slid over her once, twice, three times, her fierce smile faltering a bit with each pass.

"The time for questions is at the end of the talk, sister," she said, raising and lowering her hand, as if Bertha could be bidden like the chattering crowd had been a moment before.

Bertha remained standing.

She had planned to be genteel, placid, nonthreatening— the way women were supposed to act, even when demanding a simple acknowledgement of their humanity. Instead, she pitched her voice loud, projecting to the back of the room as her father had taught her. Years on the theater circuit meant her enunciation was crisp and sharp enough to cut to the heart of the matter.

"That's well and good, but I think I'll ask mine now, thank you," Bertha said. "You mention church and clubs and lodges and leagues, but what of the women who belong to no such organizations? What of the poor laundress, the illiterate maid, the downtrodden prostitute?" A gasp went through the crowd then, as if that last word had sucked the respectability out of the room.

"Well, our first priority is making sure that the people in a position to influence the upcoming election know what to do," Delta said. There was challenge in her tone, as if Bertha was ruining everything just by asking to be seen. "We have limited time and resources and where we direct them is of the essence."

That's that, then.

Bertha had been looking at Delta, but now angled herself toward the crowded auditorium, making eye contact with several women as she continued. "These women need the protections the right to vote will provide more than anyone. They should be a priority." She realized her righteousness was leading her off track and tried to get back to what she had come to say. She'd had a plan. "Disregarding women who aren't seen as rich, or smart, or respectable enough is a miscalculation. How can their skills be harnessed? How can they be included now, so they aren't left behind later?"

The women in the audience looked anywhere but at her. The floor, the stage, or at the women beside them as they whispered behind their hands.

"This is really not the forum for such matters," Delta said, her color high. "Once we win the right to vote for all women, we'll be able to better use our power to uplift—"

"Uplift? You mean the same patronizing lies women have been fed by men for generations? That we've been fed by Whites since the end of the war?" Bertha let out a bark of a laugh as she began making her way out of her row, her skirts grazing the knees of the scandalized women closest to her. She didn't know why she had wasted her day trying to fit in with these women.

She got to the aisle and turned back to the stage. "Keep your uplift, Mrs. Henderson. I wasn't asking how you could help these women, but how they—we—could help you. If you couldn't figure that out, then we have nothing else to discuss."

She didn't march out of the room, but walked slowly,

confidently, her hips swinging slightly too wide for good taste. As she was heading out the door, one person began clapping. Her head swiveled in their direction to meet their derision, but when she saw who it was, she realized it wasn't mockery. Seated in the back row, wearing a full-length fur coat and a smart hat that Bertha was sure cost more than she could imagine, was Miss Q, reigning queen of the numbers game. Miss Q hadn't dressed to accommodate the sensibilities of the suffragettes. When you were as powerful as her, you didn't have to.

Miss Q spoke out against social injustice and unfair conditions, and she didn't mince words. Anyone who had seen her ads demanding police reform and community improvement in the Negro newspapers knew that. Bertha nodded in the woman's direction as she passed through the door, and Miss Q nodded back, a smirk on her face.

Bertha kept her same measured pace as she walked out of the building, and as she walked blindly down the crowded streets, tilting her head at people who called out her name. She was perfectly calm and pleasant, save for the helpless anger that was only expressed in the exaggerated sway of her hips, and how tightly her gloved fists were clenched.

The sun was lowering in the sky—her entire day had been lost to the beauty salon, all to make herself presentable, but flat hair and a stuffy dress hadn't changed who she was. There was no time for rest, either. It was straight to the Cashmere to begin preparing for the Saturday evening crowd. She would have to make sure the performances were lined up perfectly to give the audience the best bang for their buck, that the food orders had come in, that the Gallucci's had delivered the ice blocks for the night, and the cops had been paid off. That her bouncers had an updated list of which men not to let inside, no matter what they said—the Cashmere had a rep for keeping its girls safe now that Bertha was in charge, and that was something she wouldn't slack on.

After doing all that, she would have to prep for her own performance. It had once been comforting to slip into her old, familiar stage persona, but just the thought of it fatigued her now. She wanted nothing more than a finger of scotch and her bed, but that wouldn't happen until the sun came up.

She entered the Cashmere through the alley that ran behind the building, using the back door that led into the kitchen.

Her chef, Cora, was already at work prepping everything she would need for the night. The woman's huge stomach poked out from beneath a now too-tight chef's jacket, reminding Bertha that she would soon need a new cook in addition to a new dishwasher.

"Has anyone stopped by, Cora?"

"Only Officer O'Donnell, looking for his envelope." She sucked her teeth. "You would think the police didn't have a payroll how often they show up here with their hands out."

Shit.

She pulled her pocket watch out and checked the time. The new dishwasher should have arrived already. When the merchant who provided her dance costumes had visited the day before to deliver a new skirt, he'd said he had a man for her. Mr. Khan was usually reliable, but if he didn't come through she was going to be in a hard spot.

"Miss Bertha?"

She breathed a sigh of relief at the sound of Ali Khan's distinct accent, a mix of Southern drawl and the lyrical cadence of his native country. She turned, allowing the brown-skinned, older man the slightest hint of a smile as she inclined her head toward him.

"Mr. Khan, how are you?" She shook his hand, as she did everyone's: brief, fast, and with enough pressure to pre-empt any they might exert on her's.

"Good, good. Heading back to New Orleans tomorrow," he said. His face lit up, and she envied him the brief burst of happiness that came from knowing he would see his wife and children soon. The man only stopped by a few times a year, but she knew everything about his family.

"I'm sure Sable and the boys are looking forward to your return."

Ali chuckled. "Sable is looking forward to having help running the shop! And maybe my esteemed presence, yes. But before that, I have another delivery for you. *Asho*, Amir."

She heard a sigh come from the proximity of the

back door, and not a wistful one. It was a sound of deep aggravation, the same she emitted before sitting down before a pile of paperwork or, lately, before donning her skirts and smile and stepping onto the stage.

The door, which had been left ajar, pushed open, and Bertha felt her control drop for just an instant. She'd expected someone young and ridiculous, or older and fatherly; just about anyone other than the dark, brooding man who stepped into the doorway with a scowl on his face.

His hair was inky black, longish and thick. It was brushed back from his face, revealing sharp cheekbones shaded by five o'clock shadow and full lips—dusky pink against his golden brown skin. His eyes were a deep, dark brown, with long lashes that seemed at odds with the intensity of his gaze. Said gaze passed over her, then away disdainfully, reminding Bertha that if she didn't constantly lay down the path for how people, men especially, treated her, they'd see her as the path itself and walk right over her.

He said something in their language to Mr. Khan, then his gaze drifted from her face to the door behind her shoulder, as if looking for someone else. She'd seen that look before; he was expecting a man to come out and talk to him.

She pursed her lips and made a show of stepping closer to him, walking a circle around him and inspecting him like a cow at the market—the same way she'd been inspected by men with promises of work when she'd shown up in New York, ready to put her past behind her and start fresh. Audition after audition, each rejection more stinging and each theater more low brow until she'd landed at an uptown cabaret, with the manager licking his lips and saying he thought she'd fit in just fine.

But that was the past. This was her joint; she was the boss now and any man who worked for her would respect that.

"Does he speak English, this Amir?" She stopped in front of him and met his gaze, letting hers dip just a bit when his lips pulled to the side in annoyance.

"He does, this Amir," came the reply, in an accent entirely different from Mr. Khan, sharpened with a crisp British enunciation. "And this Miss Hines? *Apni Bangla bolte paren?*"

"Amir," Ali said, shooting him a quelling look. "Miss Hines is a fine woman. *Bhadrobhabey kotha bolo onar shathey.*"

"Are we going to have a problem?" she asked. She could have asked herself the same thing. Her interest in men had been primarily business, even now that her business had become selling drinks and entertainment instead of her body. There had always been a sort of detachment, even when she fell apart in a man's arms—even when the men weren't paying. She had stopped dating entirely since taking over the Cashmere. Nights on the town had developed a different edge of tension; she'd often felt like a plump chicken out with a hungry farmer, never sure when he'd reveal his knife. She didn't need a man trying to cut in on her business, and she'd had more than enough of being told what to do. The only men who interested her now were the Cashmere's customers and the dead presidents on the scratch they handed her.

This Amir, though. The fact that she hadn't yet kicked him out proved she would have to be very careful with him.

That tempting mouth of his pulled up into a smile, but his eyes were still as hard as stone. "You won't have any problems from me. Just tell me what I need to do—in English—and I'll do it."

"I'll hold you to that," she said. She took another step toward him, just to see him frown again. They weren't close enough to dance, but she felt a pleasant tingle go through her at even that proximity.

Careful.

"Will you have a problem handling any particular food products?" she asked. "Beef?"

His brows went up a little, then receded back down into his glower. "I'm Muslim, not Hindu. I can't imagine eating pork is a job requirement, so as I said, no problems from me."

His response was curt, his shoulders and neck tensed as if he were straining against some challenge. She tried not to take it personally. Men always seemed to think she was challenging them, just by operating in a world outside the one located under their thumb. She kept her expression bland, letting her gaze flick over him assessingly as the silence dragged out one beat, then another.

"Well, let me know ahead of time if you need accommodation for fasting, prayer, or anything else that might come up," she said. Something struck her then. "You know what this place is, yes?"

He opened his mouth and closed it, and his gaze dropped to the ground.

He knew.

"It's a business," she continued, "and if you have a problem with any aspect of my business, let me know now. I don't want to be out a dishwasher in the middle of dinner service if you suddenly find your feathers ruffled by a girl in a short dress."

His gaze came up to meet hers, and there was that burning, insolent look again. "I need work."

"And I need a worker. It seems we have come to an agreement."

She held out her hand and he took it; he didn't try to crush her hand as she imagined he might, but waited to see how much pressure she exerted and exerted the exact same amount back. Warmth surged through her at the press of his palm against hers, delicious, unexpected, and unwanted. She squeezed a bit harder, then pulled her hand away, embarrassed at the sheen of sweat forming on her upper lip. It must have been the heat from the stove.

"Cora can you show him what to do real quick?" she asked.

"Sure," Cora said, breezily. "Not like I have a busy night to prep for."

"I have some bangles for you to look at before I go," Ali said, drawing her attention back to him. "They're very nice, and reserved for my clients in New Orleans, so you can be the only woman in New York with them!"

"You bring me the most exciting things," she said, glancing at Amir. He turned to face Cora. "Come to my office and let's see what you've got."

Ali talked about something or other as they made their way through the club and then the hall that led to her office, but Bertha wasn't listening hard. She was busy hoping the fact that her hand still tingled something fierce didn't mean a damn thing.

chapter two

Amir didn't know why he'd let Ali talk him into this. He'd told the man he was done with restaurants, after being fired from his last three jobs. He loved working in a kitchen, but it seemed employers didn't like it very much when you pointed out the unsafe, unfair, or indecent ways in which they treated their employees. The British officers aboard the *Kandahar* hadn't liked it, and the head chef at the Drake Hotel had liked it even less.

Amir stepped back as dishwater sloshed over the side of the sink, then sighed. He had always been considered *theta*, and his parents had warned that his willfulness would get him in trouble one day. His willfulness had gotten him to America, and if this country wasn't trouble, he didn't know what was.

He felt swindled, like a child who had listened to *rupkatha* before bed and come to believe the stories were real. But Amir now knew that virtue wasn't always rewarded and evil sometimes did win the day. He'd witnessed it as his family's land had diminished, plot by plot, victim of East India Company law. He'd seen it in Calcutta, in the faces of the poor on the street and the illiterate sailors who filled the boarding houses.

America was supposed to be different.

You should just go back. Like a dog, with his tail between his legs.

When he'd left his village for the port city of Calcutta, drawn by the possibility of work on a British steamer and tales of adventure and prosperity in far-away places, people had expected that he'd soon return humbled and ready to take a wife and settle on the family farmland. It wasn't that they wished him ill. It was simply that they'd seen so many of the other men who spent years in Calcutta, building up debt to the *ghat sharengs* who housed them and the *sharengs* who were the key to getting hired for an outgoing crew, return in the same manner.

But Amir hadn't been deterred. He'd grown up with stories from Raahil *Chacha*, who had made Amir study English grammar and learn about men with strange names like Marx and Engels while his cousins played. His uncle had left Bengal for adventure, despite the academic success that had already laid the foundation for a promising future. His family had considered it a betrayal, but Raahil had seen places like Morocco and Portugal and England with his own eyes, tasted their foods and mingled with their people. He told Amir all kinds of stories, except for the ones that would explain the burns on his arms and why he sometimes went quiet for days. Raahil's stories had driven Amir from his town in search of more.

In Calcutta, he'd gotten a job in a restaurant near the docks and immersed himself in the community of seamen, first teaching the illiterate men at his boarding house the basics of reading and writing and eventually, in a series of events composed of happenstance and Allah's will, organizing against unfair conditions. He'd fallen in with a group of young Socialists, drawn to them by the ideas that his *Chacha* had instilled in him. He hadn't meant to get involved in such activities, but watching the injustice that surrounded him everywhere in the crowded port city spurred him to help where he could. After two years of such work, he'd been assigned to the crew of the *Kandahar*, likely so he would no longer be a bother to the *ghat sharengs* as they grifted money from desperate men.

They certainly don't seem to mind that you never came back. While the *sharengs* did not seem to feel his loss, his family did. His cousins with no land of their own had taken the management of his, but the longer he stayed away, the murkier the situation became. In the last few weeks, Amir had begun to wonder if perhaps it wasn't time for him to return.

When he'd jumped ship in New York, fed up with the hellish conditions the British thought suitable for their Indian crewmen, he'd thought he'd make something of himself in America. He'd been on the ships for three years, and each time they stopped in New York he'd felt the city thrum in his blood. To a village boy raised on a smallholding farm in Bengal, the tall buildings and seething streets had been like walking through a dream he hadn't remembered having, even after the glorious hustle and bustle of Calcutta. He had been sure that New York was a place where he could make something of himself—outside the bounds of the British imperialist box—and return triumphant. He would buy back the plots of land his family had been forced to sell in increments as the zamindars collected their debts, and use his American-made wealth to thumb his nose at the *sahebs* and their rules.

But here he was, two years later, working the lowest job possible in a place of ill repute. The women passing in and out of the kitchen in their make-up and revealing dresses were certainly selling something more than drinks, and music and shouts filled the entire place, growing louder as the night progressed. Bertha had stopped in and told him if any strange White men tried to enter through the back door to come get her immediately, leaving him on edge and worried about raids that could have him on a boat back to Bengal. What had he gotten himself into?

One who goes to Laanka turns into Ravaan, his neighbor had chided at the celebration before he left for Calcutta, and his aunties had agreed. If they could see the company he kept now, they'd quickly join his parents in the afterlife, just to pass on news of his shame.

"Chicken fried steak, order up!" Cora called out. He looked over at the cook as she wiped sweat away from her brow and moved on to the next dish, her belly bumping the plate she'd set on the counter. Perspective coated the burn of his irritation, calming him. It chafed to be demoted to a dish scrubber while the tools of his trade were at hand, but at least he wasn't carrying a live, kicking thing in his belly while doing the work. Besides, he needed the money.

He'd been steadily building his savings, despite a few setbacks, after the last of which his enraged boss had threatened to report him as an undocumented alien—the recent immigration act had given many men a trump card over him, something Amir resented keenly. He had left Bengal to find himself and America had told him what he was: "undesirable." In the eyes of the American people, he was no different than a criminal or beggar. An exotic disease that might infect the country from within. He couldn't vote, own land, or naturalize; his life was dependent on people deciding not to report him or taking the risk of hiring him. He thought back to the way Bertha had looked down her nose at him, though he'd felt something other than resentment stir in him then.

Na, Amir. There was no point in thinking about her full lips pressing together as she'd inspected him like one of the British officers before he'd boarded their ships. When Ali Khan had told him what kind of place the Cashmere was and that it was owned by a woman, he'd expected someone frivolous, gaudy; it hadn't even registered to him that the woman in the kitchen could be her. He'd thought her just another witness to his shame. But Bertha Hines had wasted no time in correcting his misconception; she had been sharp, all business.

Except for the way she looked at your mouth. Remember that?

Amir did remember. He also remembered the way she had been so close that the scent of her hair had enveloped him, heavy floral musk tucked up primly under that hat of hers. And though he had balked at the way she brought up his religion—as if it would stop him from doing his job—in retrospect, he realized that she was the only employer who had even taken it seriously. He ran his hands over his apron, feeling a different kind of shame at how he'd taken each question as a challenge and reacted accordingly.

Patha! Stubborn ram, always looking for something to butt his head against. His father had roughed a hand through Amir's hair each time he repeated what became a common saying in the family, even after he'd needed to reach his hand up to do it. Amir missed that, even though he'd often jerked away, indignant.

His flatmates called him Pintu, but it wasn't the same. No one in America knew that *daak naam*. *Patha* was buried with his parents.

Across the kitchen, Cora huffed and put a hand to her stomach. She had been frowning in concentration since the dinner service had started a few hours before, but now a smile illuminated her face.

"Strong kicker?" Amir ventured. Her head whipped in

his direction, but then she dropped her hand and went back to work. She'd eyed him suspiciously since he'd interrupted her training for the Maghrib prayer, making Amir wish he'd asked Bertha where he could do so in private when she had offered. He sighed and sloshed another pan into the soapy water.

"Feels like he's tryin' to kick me to the moon sometimes," Cora said after a long silence.

Amir smiled, remembering when Sabiha Auntie had been pregnant with his cousin and let him feel the baby move beneath his hand. Amaan was all grown up now, working in the fire room of a British ship, last he'd heard. On the *Kandahar*, one fireman had gone mad from the heat and attacked one of the officers, who'd tried to force him back into the inferno of the engine room. It had made Amir wonder about those days when Raahil Uncle had sat slack-mouthed and blank-eyed, staring into the distance.

"That means he's anxious to get out and show the world what he can do," Amir said as he scrubbed. "He'll be a go-getter, as they say."

Cora chuckled. "If he's anything like my husband Darryl, that's a sure thing. Fried chicken and greens, order up!"

They worked in silence for a bit, Amir scrubbing glasses and shoving them into drying racks as Cora bustled about the kitchen. Each time she passed him, he felt a bit more like an ass. He dropped the last glass into the rack and wiped his hands on his apron.

"I have experience working in a kitchen. Tell me what to do, and you can rest for a bit. Do you need anything prepped?"

She narrowed her eyes at him, and he could tell she was struggling with giving him even a bit of control over her workspace. He'd never been able to do it in his kitchens, but Cora had extenuating circumstances that he'd never had to consider.

"I was a cook back home, and on a ship, and since I've been here in the States," he said. "I learned at the side of a man who would not think twice about throwing a hot pan in your direction if you made a mistake and I won't even tell you how strict my grandmother was. I won't make a mess of things, if you tell me how you want it done."

Cora bit her lip, then glanced at the pile of greens beside the cutting board. "You ever made collards?"

Amir smiled; his flatmates would get a laugh out of a Bong being asked if he could cook *shak*. Slightly less insulting than asking if he could cook fish. He still remembered following his *Nani* through the market each morning, as she bought whatever was cheap and in season, and then into the kitchen as she decided the best way to prepare it. He'd learned at the knee of a master culinary improviser. But Cora had no reason to know that, and he had jumped to enough conclusions for one night. Besides, a good cook was always looking to improve.

"Can you show me?"

ɔ ɔ ɔ

Amir watched the plate the waitress carried out of the kitchen with more than a bit of pride. He was an accomplished cook, but this Southern style food wasn't something he'd tried before. Cora had tasted the fried chicken and collards herself, giving him a nod of approval, and then sat down and eaten some during her break. Amir had a small plate of the *shak* at her urging, and was proud of his attempt. The greens were tender and tangy, infused with a hint of the smoked turkey neck Cora had told him to add for flavor instead of the ham hocks that were part of her own recipe. The chicken was crisp, the combination of spices a perfect complement to the succulent meat beneath. It wasn't halal, but Amir's philosophy held that Allah was more forgiving of certain transgressions. On payday, he would head to the kosher butcher, the closest thing to halal, and make a feast for his flatmates. With a bit of *panch phoron* mixed into the seasoned flour coating, the chicken would be even better.

He was contemplating variations on Cora's recipe when a sound that seemed distinctly out of place at the Cashmere reached his ears. He still wasn't used to the loud music, but most of it had been enjoyable enough that it had him tapping his feet or moving his head in time. He hadn't expected this.

He stood, drawn toward the main section of the club by the familiar sound of fingers plucking skillfully at the taut strings of a sitar, the blows of palms against a tabla setting a driving percussive beat. Those were the sounds of home, coming from the stage of this Harlem hole in the wall.

He got to the door and stopped. Dishwashers weren't allowed out front at most places, and he was sure the Cashmere was no exception.

"Go ahead and peek," Cora said. "Nobody gonna be looking this way now. Not while Miss Hines is up there."

He pushed the door open a crack and was surprised to see some White faces in the crowd, along with the varying shades of brown. That was no small thing, given the way segregation was so strictly enforced in the States. Cora was correct: the women with their sleek hair and the men in their sharp suits, all of them were staring toward the front of the club, enraptured. He pressed the door open a bit more so that the stage came into view and he saw exactly why.

Cora had said it was Bertha on the stage, but for a moment Amir knew she had to be wrong. A woman clad in an elegant sari stood there, her long, dark hair falling over her shoulder in waves and her arms curving up and over her head. Her stance meant that her cropped choli was lifted perilously high, revealing bare brown skin from her waist to approximately three rib bones short of *Jannah*. Beneath the flowing fabric of her loose skirt, one dainty foot was on point. Her knee was bent and pressing against the skirt in a way that somehow made you quite aware that it was bare skin pressing against smooth fabric. She just stood there, drawing it out until Amir found himself willing her to move.

When the tension in the room was about to teeter into unbearable, she turned her head abruptly toward the audience, teasing, just as her hips began to sway. Her eyes were lined with dark kohl, making them seem large and enticing. Her lips were red, luscious, but the smile that rested on them was relaxed and mysterious.

Jewelry was draped over her hair and encircling her forehead, sparkling gold to match the earrings that dripped from her ears, the temple necklace that circled over her collarbones, and the bangles that lined her wrists.

The plucking of the sitar strings began to pick up pace and Bertha launched fully into her dance. Amir watched, annoyance, amusement, and something dangerously close to lust swirling in his mind as she whirled before him. The dance was delicate and feminine and powerful all at once, but more than anything it was seductive. What it was *not,* was an actual Indian dance.

Most classical dance was rooted in Hinduism, but Amir's village had been one in which religion had generally been no barrier to friendship and community; he had learned classical dance from neighborhood festivities and annual celebrations with friends, and this wasn't it. There were bits and pieces mashed together—she completed some mudras, striking the hand poses fairly accurately; others were things he supposed she had created on her own. He could see hints of ballet in the way she jumped and swayed, and he supposed other styles were mixed in too. Her arms moved languidly, and her feet followed familiar patterns—to an outsider she looked like she knew what she was doing. Her shoulders jumped and her bangles shook in time to the music. But the way she moved her hips was something entirely American.

The day before Amir had boarded the *Kandahar*, he had come across a street performance near the docks in Calcutta. An old woman beside him had huffed, "Nachinir lajja nei dekhunir lajja." *The dancer isn't ashamed, but the onlooker is.* He was definitely not ashamed as he watched Bertha, though other sentiments stirred in him. He should have been offended at yet another bastardization of his culture, but he felt a kind of wonder as she whirled and swayed. Perhaps it was because the woman on the stage was so open and free, compared to the stiff-backed woman he'd met in the kitchen.

He'd seen *baiji* women perform their dances for the *sahebs* in Calcutta, had also seen the *sahebs* demand to be taught in one breath and decry the dances as repulsive and lewd with the next. He scorned the British for taking every bit of his culture and steeping it in their own ways until it was to their taste, dashing out what wasn't. But watching Bertha elicited something else in him. Something that made his heart race and also hit him with a wave of homesickness stronger than the sea churned by the rage of a monsoon.

He felt Cora come stand beside him but he couldn't tear his gaze away from the woman on the stage. The same woman who'd talked down to him like he was a cur who had wandered in from the alley, begging for a scrap of meat. Amir considered that perhaps he had been wrong to be offended by her show of superiority earlier: he and every other person in the audience were quite ready to prostrate themselves before her as she whirled toward the finale of the song.

"She don't perform as much anymore since she took over the place," Cora whispered. "But I sure love when she does."

Bertha spun into a dramatic pose, back bent, hands supplicant, dark-rimmed eyes turned towards the heavens as if she begged for redemption. The music stopped and the audience went wild, cheering and hooting, begging for an encore.

Bertha finally left her pose and graced the crowd with a smile. Someone handed her a microphone, and she spoke in that velvety voice of hers that had stroked over Amir during their first encounter.

"Thank you, everyone, for coming to the Cashmere tonight. We've got a ragtime group from Louisiana up after this intermission, so I hope I'll see you all dancing yourselves. Especially you over there, with those rubber legs of yours." Amir couldn't see who she extended her arm toward, but low laughter rumbled through the crowd. "I do have a special message for all of the men in the crowd, tonight," she said. Her voice dropped low, husky, and every man in the crowd leaned closer, as if she were talking to him and him alone. Amir did, too, then leaned back, annoyed that he could be taken in by her ploy. He watched the hungry expressions of the men closest to him, and felt a serpentine motion inside of him that had nothing—or everything—to do with how Bertha's sinuous hips had entranced him.

"Fellas," she said, voice intimate like she was speaking to her lover across a pillow. "Did you enjoy my dance tonight?"

The crowd broke out into more hoots, hollers, and whistles.

"Why'd you make us wait so long for it?" a man called out, followed by a chorus of agreement.

She smiled, her gaze slipping in the direction of the outburst, then to the ground, all coyness. Amir felt himself leaning toward her again, and he didn't fight it this time.

"Oh, you want me to dance again?" she asked.

More shouts, more applause, and then she lifted her head and pinned the crowd with a look that made Amir's throat go tight and his pulse race.

"Remember that when you go to the ballot box one month from now. Because I've got a hankering to vote and the only one who can help with that is you men. Vote yes for women's suffrage, because until she gets the right to vote, this nautch girl is retired."

She capped her statement with a wink, and then sauntered backstage, ignoring the incredulous shouts interspersed with laughter that followed in her wake. Men jumped up in their seats and women reached across tables to touch fingertips with their friends as they shared knowing looks. Amir simply stared at the curtain that had closed behind her.

"Ain't she something?" Cora hooted, slapping Amir's shoulder.

"Yes," Amir responded. "Something, indeed."

chapter three

"I still don't understand why we have to be here today. I'm still exhausted from Saturday." Janie crossed her arms on the table directly in front of the stage and rested her head on it. Her face was clean, make-up free, reminding Bertha that she was younger than she appeared when she was glammed up and working the crowd. Janie was always exhausted, but that was to be expected when a girl had a movie star face and an hour glass figure to match. Her services were always in demand, both at the Cashmere and with the sugar daddies she had in rotation outside the club's walls.

"We're here today because the vote is happening less than a month from now," Bertha said, pacing back and forth on the stage. "I'm glad you decided to show up this time. I got up early the other day and you all stood me up."

Wah Ming, who went by Jade to the men at the club who were flummoxed by two simple syllables, brushed her blunt bangs out of her eyes before lighting the cigarette

Janie had just rolled for her. "That's because you scheduled it for the morning after a party with all the Tammany bigwigs. We were beat!"

"That you all are invited to these kinds of parties is one reason why I'm giving these courses," Bertha said. "Look, I've told you already, the vote will be here before we know it. Any man who isn't absolutely voting yes has to be convinced otherwise."

From the corner of her eye, she saw the kitchen door open half way. Amir's head popped through and he held up a hand in greeting. She'd asked him to come in and do some repair work if he wanted to take home a bit more money. He'd been obliging, shockingly so, considering the way he'd squared off with her when he first arrived. After that first day, he'd been reserved with her but not sullen. Cora seemed sweet on him after a few shifts together, a first for the Cashmere kitchen. He was a good worker, and that was all that mattered, anyway; everyone knew Bertha Hines didn't play in her own yard, or anyone's yard, when it came down to it.

Some said she did it to keep men panting after her, which was partially true. Men wanted nothing more than what they couldn't have, and if that kept them coming to the Cashmere, that was fine with her. But after years of being groped up and put down, Bertha mostly wanted peace of mind.

She chucked her chin in Amir's direction to acknowledge him and he slipped back into the kitchen.

"I'm no suffragette," a woman from the back called out, saying the word the same way most suffragettes would refer to her profession. She received grumbles of approval from the small crowd of girls Bertha hired as waitresses—and rented her back rooms to for their other work, with the offer of protection.

Bertha sighed. "Do you want laws that protect you from the police officers who hit you up for bribes? From the people who won't hire you for jobs and never gave you the opportunity for schooling?"

There was a sulky silence in the room but no dissent, and Bertha smiled. "Then you are suffragettes. We need to get this vote and we need to know what to do with it once we have it. Today we'll be going over local government and a few recent laws that have had a negative impact on you."

"Like the hotel law?" Janie asked sleepily. The law had been passed to make it harder for prostitutes to rent rooms, meaning more women had to hustle on the streets or give up their earnings to pimps.

"Yes, like that. We'll examine who voted for the laws and what political parties they come from." Bertha felt the slightest spark of hope. "Now, none of you are fools. I've seen you hold conversations with every type of man in the Apple, from shoe shiners to senators. There's no reason you shouldn't have some say in what happens in this city and this country."

"No one cares what we think," another woman, Cathy, called out. "Half these suffragettes think we dragging down the race. Way they tell it, if we just dressed nice and stopped whoring around, people would treat us right."

"And I still won't be allowed to vote, even if women get suffrage," Wah Ming added. "Remember? My kind isn't wanted here." She stubbed her cigarette out into an ashtray.

Bertha understood their frustration; when the decks were stacked against you, playing felt futile. "Many people would be glad if none of us in this room existed, and if we never got the right to vote. That would work out real nice for them, wouldn't it? If we never had the chance to take them to task for treating us like shit?"

She took a deep breath. Cussing aloud wasn't part of the image of control she tried to project, but it had many of the girls sitting up and paying attention.

"But what if we get the vote and nothing changes?" someone asked. The voice was so quiet it could have been the nagging one that kept her up at night. Bertha looked at the women before her; some were happy with their lot in life, some were not. The majority had not been given much of a choice. All had lived with disappointment as a constant companion; such was the fate of any woman in the United States, and especially ones born some shade darker than porcelain white.

"If we get the vote, everything will already have changed," Bertha said. "And once we have it, we'll keep voting until we get every damn thing we deserve from this country." She let the words hang there. "We fight in a hundred ways just to get through every day. Let's see what happens when we try fighting one hundred and one, okay?"

Bertha looked out at the women, not sure if she'd let her natural flair for the dramatic push them too far, too fast.

"You know, I used to pull some good grades before I had to leave school," Janie said. "I guess a couple more lessons wouldn't hurt none."

"Good. Let's get started."

෴ ෴ ෴

Later that day, Bertha sat at her desk reading through the local Negro newspapers she hadn't had time to peruse earlier in the week. Her office was decorated in soothing colors: warm pink and yellow fabrics, souvenirs from her time spent on the road. None of the familiar objects worked to calm the tension that mounted as she read. A letter from her mother in Chicago, with news of her brothers and step-father, had already left her feeling sad, an emotion she generally pretended didn't exist. Then she'd seen one of the regular ads from Ms. Q in *The Age*:

To the Black citizens of Harlem: On Tuesday, October 5, 1917, three women were beaten and robbed by officers of the law. This was carried out in plain daylight and nothing will be done because these women also sell their bodies. Those of you who look down on such things will say they deserved it, while your husbands will be wondering if it was one of the women they are stepping out on you with. Regardless of what you think of their profession, these women have rights. To the men reading this, stop spending your time scheming to get women in your bed and think on how to get them to the ballot box. Give women the right to vote against politicians who allow things like this to happen unchecked.

Bertha was glad for the ad, written in Ms. Q's signature style, but distressed about what it reported. When she turned the page she was met with even worse news. Two more clubs in the neighborhood had been shut down over allegations of prostitution and racial mixing. One was going to reopen, and the owner of the other remained jailed.

She dropped the paper down onto the pile of invoices and receipts that constituted the afternoon bookkeeping, pushing her palms into her eyes as frissons of panic ran through her body and coalesced at the back of her neck.

Why can't they just leave us be?

When the Commission of Fourteen had started, their primary goal had been stopping "White slavery," or what they called White prostitution. Now, seemingly bored after helping drive Negroes up the length of Manhattan all the way to Harlem, the vice squad had decided to target them, too. Not out of any desire to stop "Black slavery"—she was sure many of the men working that beat weren't put out by that particular moral failing—but for two reasons: to shut down Negro businesses and to stop White folks from patronizing them. A couple of them had come sniffing around the Cashmere over the past few months, and unlike the beat cops, they seemed immune to bribery. Bertha could almost laugh; between the suffragettes and the vice squad, the primary function of morality seemed to be as a thorn in her side.

Most of the other clubs had already put in strict "No Whites" policies. While it should have been slightly edifying to be able to wield such power, it wasn't done out of hatred. It was the only surefire way to avoid investigation, and for their owners to avoid jail time.

It was all so ridiculous.

Bertha, perhaps more than most, understood how

subjective a thing race was. She looked up at the framed poster on the wall beside her desk and sighed.

THE RAJJAH BEN SPECTACULAR

FAR EASTERN MYSTICAL MAGIC NEVER SEEN ON THESE SHORES! MIND READING, SPIRIT SUMMONING, AND OTHER ACTS OF LEGERDEMAIN! HINDOO DANCING, AND MORE!

A knock at the door cut her moment of pity short.

All for the better, she thought.

"Come in," she called out, straightening in her seat. The door opened and Amir stepped through. He wore a simple tan shirt, tucked neatly into dark trousers paired with suspenders. His sleeves were rolled up to his elbows, and Bertha tried hard not to stare at the sleek, dark hair that dusted over his forearms and peeked out of the neckline of his shirt.

"Can I help you, Amir?"

"May I sit?" he asked.

She nodded and he settled into the seat in front of her desk. She tried to read his expression to determine whether he was going to quit, demand a raise, or try to give her some friendly advice, as men were wont to do.

"I listened to your talk earlier," he said, then stopped abruptly. She waited for him to go on, but he shifted in his seat and began looking around the office.

"Is there some reason you feel compelled to tell me about your eavesdropping?" Her voice came out low, flirtatious, even though that wasn't what she intended at all. It made her feel a bit strange to know he'd been listening, which was ridiculous because performing on stage was second nature to her. But she hadn't been performing, really. She'd let her guard down for a moment, as she joked and traded information with the women, who had by the end seemed as excited with the project as she was.

"It's just...why are you doing this?"

She would have been offended if the expression on his face hadn't been so direct. There was no judgment or, worse, disgust, but you never could tell. Maybe it bothered him to see women learning about politics. That would be more likely than him supporting it, given most men she'd encountered.

His dark gaze was fixed on her with the same intensity as their first meeting, but without the frustrated anger— she realized now that's what it had been. Her face heated under his scrutiny.

"Well, I want the women to be prepared when we get the right to vote," she said. "It may not happen a month from now, but it will happen soon."

She didn't mention how she knew so much about the law. As they'd traveled from state to state and city to city, her father had always made sure they knew the local and federal ordinances that could help or hurt them in case things went sideways. What was allowed for Negroes, what was allowed for women, what the local government and police forces were like.

Gotta know the lay of the land before you take the shortcut, Bertie.

"No. *That* was incredible. I understand why you teach the class." He leaned forward in his seat. "I'm asking why do you do *this*." He spread his arms expansively. "I admit I don't know very much about politics here, outside of certain specific things I've learned the hard way, but you know so much. Why run this club? If you are interested in helping these women, why allow them to sell themselves?"

The words pelted Bertha like fruit thrown from a balcony. She pursed her lips as she tried to gauge how much she felt like explaining the ways of a woman's world to a man, and found she didn't feel like it at all.

She leaned back in her seat. "I won't be questioned about my business by a dishwasher. You can go."

She picked up the paper on her desk and stared at it, eyes blindly scanning. After a few moments of silence, she glanced up over the edge of the paper to find him watching her. His gaze swept her face, as if trying to figure her out; she'd seen him look at a clogged drain with the same pensiveness. Bertha didn't take to being puzzled over.

"You've been dismissed, Amir."

"I think perhaps there has been some misunderstanding," he said. "I asked because I want to know, not as an insult. I apologize for hurting you."

"You should apologize for thinking someone like you *could* hurt me," she said, letting the paper flop onto her desk ever so casually and smiling at him as if that were the silliest idea she'd ever heard.

That was usually enough to put a man in his place, but Amir didn't even flinch.

"So if I told you your dance the other day was a sad imitation of the real thing, it wouldn't bother you in the least?" he parried, his smile just as benign. It quickly faded, as did Bertha's brief hit of pleasure from taking a jab at him.

She'd been insulted in many ways, but never about her dancing. That had been the one thing that no one—not her father, not the racist audiences, not the theater directors who had deemed her style "unpolished" during audition after audition—had been able to make her doubt. To most people, her dance had been some exotic fantasy and she had excelled at it; Amir knew better, and he found it *sad*. She would have taken anything else: ungainly, graceless, lewd. Sad? Bertha had been ambivalent about her dancing lately, but she still had her pride.

He stood up suddenly, scrubbing a hand over his face. "I shouldn't have said that. You know, I came in here because I thought maybe we could help each other, but obviously I was wrong. I finished the repairs to those chairs like you wanted. Good day."

"Wait." Bertha was standing now, too, fingertips

pressing into the edge of her desk. He'd apologized for his words, but that was different from saying he didn't mean them. "It's rude to offer a blanket critique and then run away. Tell me specifically what you found so sad."

He exhaled through his nose. "Well, I suppose this won't be the strangest way I've ever been fired," he muttered, shaking his head. "You dance wasn't sad. I was being spiteful because you made me angry."

"You'll agree that's one thing I seem to do well."

He let out a short laugh, and Bertha realized that he had a deep indentation in each cheek. It was the first time she had noticed, and she hoped it would be the last given the sudden flush that went through her body.

"I wanted to suggest a trade," he said. "I know your class is for your women, but I wondered if I could listen in from the kitchen during each session. I learned a lot, things I don't learn from my flatmates—we're usually talking about the politics back home."

He paused, pressed his lips together in the way stubborn people did when forced to give up something they didn't want to. "I came to America for the opportunity. Then I got here and everything I see is oppression. I have no rights and no hope of them unless something changes. I need to learn."

It was the yearning in his voice that got her. The hopeless desire for more that got stomped out of every American with any good sense after a while, replaced with hatred or defeat or going along to get along. Bertha had just discovered that yearning again, and she wasn't going to be the one to kill it in Amir.

"You can listen without offering me anything in return. Good day." She sat down, sighing around the lingering sting of his insult. It would fade, as all bruises did.

"I don't take charity," he said, shoving his hands into his pockets. "I can teach you some things about dance in exchange."

He was looking down at her, a glint in his eyes that made her neck go warm, again. Being closer to Amir was the last thing she needed and dance lessons would necessitate exactly that.

"A dancer and a dishwasher, how remarkable," she said. "No thank you."

"For someone who just got done telling those women not to let the world look down on them, you seem very preoccupied with the position you hired me for," he stated calmly. "I'm sure you know this, but power dynamics rooted in social status are a system designed to separate people instead of bringing them together for the greater good."

Bertha raised a brow. She didn't feel shame at the reprimand; derision was often the only weapon she had. She had the uncomfortable feeling that Amir might understand that.

"My very own Bolshevik," she said, tilting her head.

"Isn't that the bee's knees."

"There are worse things I could be," he said. "A Democrat. Or is it Republicans who push these restrictive laws on Colored people? If only I had someone to instruct me in such things."

His thumbs slid behind the straps of his suspenders and he looked at her in a manner she figured was charming, if you liked dimples and full lips and raised brows.

She picked up a stack of papers on her desk and began leafing through them. "The next lesson is in two days. You can tutor me directly after."

chapter four

Amir had spent the morning before the first lesson pretending it was just a regular day, but his flatmates had sensed something amiss, peering at him curiously as he sipped his *cha* and read letters from home, updating him on family friends, his land, and local politics.

"What is it?" Fayaz had finally asked, his dark brows drawn together as he rubbed a palm over the morning stubble covering his round cheeks. He'd pulled off a bit of the puffy wheat *luchi* Amir had made and dipped it into the fragrant *aloo dum*, using it to scoop up the potatoes, onions, and garlic that comprised their simple breakfast. "Did the Hines woman finally kick you out on your bottom? You have more than enough savings to get by, don't worry so much."

"No, no. It's something else," Syed had cut in, getting up to stand next to Amir and lean in close, examining him. "Starched shirt with a clean collar. He's got *pomatum* in his hair, he's shaved, and he doesn't smell like a donkey's behind for once. Hmm…"

Amir swatted at Syed, who jogged just out of reach and pointed at him, eyes wide and brows raised. "He's going to see a woman!"

Amir downed the rest of his tea and stood up, ignoring his laughing friends as he carried his cup to the sink. "I have an assignment at work today. I criticized my boss's dancing, see"—he waited for the groans and recriminations of his flatmates to subside— "and then I told her I could teach her a thing or two."

There was silence behind him as he washed his cup, and he braced himself for a barrage of jibes and jokes at his expense. When he was done washing and drying and the jokes hadn't commenced, he turned to find Fayaz and Syed staring at him.

"You're going to dance?" Syed had asked.

"We could barely get you to dance *jari* last month," Fayaz had said. "I thought you were so shy, and now you're teaching someone?"

"A female someone, who had his brow creased like old *roti* the morning after he came back from his first shift," Syed had added. He and Fayaz had chuckled conspiratorially.

"It's nothing. She's teaching me what she knows about politics and I'm teaching her what I know about dancing. It's a mutual exchange of skills, nothing more. I thought you both were socialists, *na*?"

Both flatmates had burst out laughing and Amir had

grabbed his coat and headed for the Cashmere. They were right; he was more of a wallflower than a dancer. He spent his time at festivities in clusters of likeminded people railing against British imperialism. That didn't mean he couldn't dance; young people dreaming of revolution were not exempt from family and religious events.

Amir had lied to Syed and Fayaz though. It wasn't *nothing*; for the first time in a long while, he had found himself looking forward to a dance. And for the first time since he was a child, he was nervous about it.

Rupe Lakshmi, gune Saraswati. That's what he had thought when he'd heard Bertha teaching the women in her employ. *Beautiful as Lakshmi, learned as Saraswati.* He worshipped neither goddess, but he wasn't sure he could say the same of Bertha if he got too close to her. And he was supposed to teach her to dance.

Now he sat in the kitchen, seat pulled up to the door as Bertha circled the stage, explaining the different branches of local elected government and what their roles were. Her hair was twisted back into two rolls that met at the nape to form a bun, leaving her strong jawline and swan-like neck exposed. Her loose blue blouse was tucked into black trousers, wherein Amir's problem laid. Her skirts were never ridiculous and frilly, but those trousers left nothing to the imagination. They clung to the curve of her behind, highlighted the flare of her hips and the taper of her thighs. Amir paid attention to her words, but while his ears were compliant, his eyes were following another course of study.

While her hips were curved, her posture was straight as a mainmast. There was no bend to her there, which was perfect for the kind of dancing he would assist her with, but his mind strayed to the more carnal ways in which she might lose that rigidity.

Thamo. He was leering after her like a pervert stalking women at market. While he was no stranger to lust, he'd thought himself better than that. He shut his eyes and exhaled.

Allah, keep my thoughts respectful and proper.

"Okay. I see some of you are falling asleep, so we'll finish here for today," Bertha said.

"Can we talk more about electing judges next time?" Janie asked. She was Amir's favorite because she always asked for explanations that he couldn't ask for himself. "Because these cops are a problem, but it's the judges who want to throw the book at you. I want to vote for someone who doesn't pretend he don't got a pecker."

Amir suppressed a laugh, but he must have made a sound because Bertha glanced at him. The corners of her mouth raised by a few degrees, and the shift in latitude did something to Amir. He lost his equilibrium for a second, like those first days onboard a ship when his body hadn't yet adjusted to the vessel riding the dips and swells of the ocean.

His will power was going to require more than a quick request for divine help, it seemed.

"Of course," Bertha said, turning back to the women.

"When I went to night court last week, I told the judge that the cops stole from my apartment and he said I was lying," a waitress named Eve said. "I bet they get a cut of what they steal from us."

"Maybe. One day when you're able to vote, you can help vote him out," Bertha said. "Okay. Those of you working tonight, be back at eight o'clock."

The women got up and filed out, some of them peeking through the propped-open kitchen door. When they had all gone and he could dawdle no longer, Amir stood and walked toward the stage, but Bertha had stepped down.

"Are we not going to…exchange now?" Amir asked. The possibility disappointed him more than he expected.

"We're going to practice in my apartment," she said.

"Don't want to be seen cavorting with the dishwasher, eh?" That possibility disappointed him more than expected, too.

"Okay, I earned that," she said. "My apartment will give us more privacy. Unless that makes you uncomfortable."

Her hand went up to her earlobe to finger the pearl set in gold that hung there, and in that motion he glimpsed something incongruous with the Bertha he'd come to know over the last few days: vulnerability. She wanted privacy because she didn't want anyone to see them, and not because of him. It did something to him, seeing that flash of uncertainty in her. It was as if she'd shared a secret with him, had revealed the soft spot she kept hidden from a world always probing for one. He cringed in memory of his arrogant appraisal of her dance.

"That's fine," he said. "But before we start, I need to make something clear."

"What's that? That you don't want me trying to sully your virtue?" The right side of her mouth lifted up, and it was so striking he was glad she hadn't deemed him worthy of a full smile. His head went fuzzy for a moment, like when he was working in a hot kitchen and forgot to eat or drink.

"I was a sailor, Miss Hines. I have very little virtue left, and you're welcome to it."

That got a light laugh from her, as if his answer surprised her.

His grin faded as he tried to broach the uncomfortable topic that had to be tackled before they began. He didn't know if it was necessary for her, but it was for him.

"Spit it out, Amir."

"Dancing can be a very personal, spiritual, cultural thing for some. It isn't for me. I can teach you some basic technical aspects, but I'm not going to be your guru." He would have had to be Hindu to be a guru anyway, but the American craze for all things "exotic" didn't care much about differences in religion, language, or caste.

She didn't say anything and he tried again, softening his words.

"I meant no offense. I know there are people paying good money for a brown man to teach them Eastern spirituality. I can't do that for you."

She let out a short, sharp laugh. "Oh, trust me, I know what people are willing to pay. Dance is all I want from you."

He resisted offering up his virtue again; she was his boss, even when she teased him. He followed her through a hallway that branched off the dance floor to its end, where she unlocked a door that led to a flight of stairs. At the top was another door, which opened to a large apartment— large compared to where he lived, at least. He slipped out of his shoes at the threshold of the door, ignoring her confused expression, to take in the space where she lived.

The furniture was all dark wood and sharp angles, which might have meant the previous owner had been a man but could just as easily have been Bertha's taste. Framed images adorned the walls, and shelves lined with books. He spotted something familiar and realized it was a variation of the poster he had seen in her office.

"Rajjah Ben," he read aloud.

She was bent over the graphophone already, a round black disc balanced delicately against her fingertips, but she paused, head tilted and eyes wide as if the dance practice had already begun and she was striking a pose.

"'Come see the mystic of the Far East and his dervish daughter,'" he continued. She dropped the disc down onto the turntable but didn't move the needle.

"Well, I guess it's best you know, especially given your little speech downstairs. I've spent half my life doing this kind of dance and still haven't added up to more than a sad imitation. Story of my life." She said the words on a faux sigh, as if they were a joke, but Amir knew better than that. There was a bitterness there that resonated in him, the same thing that vibrated in his marrow and bones when he joked about tea time or wearing his shoes in the house.

He kept his eyes on her, on that back so straight it might buckle from the strain. "If you were the dervish daughter, then Rajjah Ben was your father."

She walked over to the couch and sat, began working at the laces of her boots. "Yes. He was a very talented musician, and a charlatan. Long story, short: he met an Indian man while performing in New Orleans, a trader like our Mr. Khan, and asked about the turban he wore and what it represented. The man told my father it represented freedom; he only wore it so Whites would leave him be when he traveled selling his goods. It was a ruse that people accepted because of the very little they knew about Indians. My father became obsessed. With the culture, with the music, with the fact that a man darker than him could travel wherever he pleased just because he was neither White nor Black."

Amir studied her face, and the careful absence of expression that told him just how deeply her father's decision had affected her.

She shrugged. "One day while traveling for a show, he bought a strip of linen, wrapped it around his head, and entered a restaurant that served Whites exclusively. He nearly sweated the thing through, way he told it, but when the manager came up to him, he asked him if he was a dignitary instead of telling him to get out. Rajjah Ben was born that day. He acquired fancier turbans, elaborate robes. An accent that would make you cringe. I'm sorry." She glanced at him to catch his reaction. Amir's neck tensed, but how could he blame her for her father's obsession? "His dervish daughter joined him a few years later, once she'd finished primary school and the dancing lessons he'd set up for her."

"And your mother?" he asked.

"My father thought she was too obviously Negro to pass, and she refused to pretend to be otherwise anyway." She shrugged. "He kept me on the road for months at a time, the stretches getting longer as I got older. One day she wrote to say she'd found a new man, one who didn't want her to be something she wasn't and who didn't pretend he was either."

The wistfulness in her voice was faint, but knowing her, it only hinted at the true depth of her pain.

"They live in Chicago now. They came to see our show with their two little boys during our final tour a while back, and I brought the boys—my brothers—onstage to participate. It was nice."

She looked at him. Amir didn't know what to say. He knew America was not fair—his own attempts to get citizenship had proven that. But the desperation that led to the creation of Rajjah Ben, and to Bertha's loss, was not unfamiliar to him.

"Back home, the change began slowly, they said," he said. "I was too young to notice, but my father railed against the men wearing British trousers and their ridiculous hats. 'Next they'll paint their faces white!' he said." He looked down. "Have you noticed my accent? How it's different from Ali Khan's?"

She nodded.

"When I got to Calcutta, a drunk saheb bumped into me. I told him to watch where he was going and he mimicked my accent, roaring with laughter." His face still heated, thinking of how ugly and shameful his words had sounded spat back at him. "I spent months getting rid of it, trying so hard to sound like the people I hated. Because I knew there was opportunity in erasing the parts of me that they found laughable."

There was a noise as she stood from the couch. Her heeled boots were gone, and it surprised him, how small she really was. Bertha didn't feel small.

"I know some people find psychoanalysis stimulating, but I'm not one of them. Shall we dance?"

Her voice was so silky smooth that it took a moment for the slap of her words to hit him. He'd never told anyone that about himself and she had brushed it away. Then he looked at how her chest rose and fell, at the way her lips pressed together, and remembered that to a ram, butting against a wall was less painful than a blow to the flank that took it unawares.

"I had an accent once, too," she finally said when he didn't respond. Then she raised her arms and cupped her hands, as if waiting for the rain to come and fill them. "Shall we dance?"

It was an order this time, but a gentle one.

He took a deep breath. "Of course. Show me what you've got."

chapter five

"Okay, lift your shoulders, *then* turn your hands like…so. Yes, like that. Press your fingers together harder. Make sure your feet hit the floor three times. Like this."

Amir executed the move he was explaining, and Bertha nodded, but mostly to the thought that was running through her head.

He's gorgeous.

This was their fourth session and it was getting harder to fight those kinds of thoughts, the ones at odds with the standards she had set for herself once she took over the Cashmere. Once she'd regained control of her own life. But Amir's shirt was off, thrown over the arm of her settee, and he stood there in his undershirt, suspenders hanging down over his trousers, and a fine sheen of sweat on his arms and face.

She tried the move again, finishing in the pose of invitation, but already knew she hadn't done it quite right by the expression on his face. He wasn't demanding, or exacting—his expression was one of indulgence. It was *kind*. She hated it.

She didn't know exactly why she had agreed to the lessons; she supposed that like Janie, she couldn't turn down the chance to see what could have happened if she'd been given proper tutelage. That, and she couldn't pass Amir every day and live with the knowledge that he'd found her lacking.

"Here, let's try this." He turned and reached into the pocket of his jacket and pulled something out, then came and knelt before her. "Put your foot on my knee."

She looked down at his thick black hair, at the whorl in the middle that would not be tamed by his pomade. She had never seen a man from this angle, she realized; she'd been with so many, but she had always been the one kneeling. An unwanted arousal bloomed in her as she lifted her bare foot and rested it on the curve of his bent leg. His kneecap poked into the sole of her foot as he shifted his weight and she let out a soft gasp. She wasn't one for soft gasps, so when he looked up at her, she was sure he saw that her brows were raised with surprise at herself.

"Ticklish?" he asked, grinning. His two front teeth were a little too large, but for some reason that only made Bertha think of how they'd feel pressing into her inner thigh.

Don't think it.

She tried to school her thoughts, but her resistance to

the images flashing in her mind didn't stop the heat dancing in her belly like Salomé. She found that she was still able to blush, after all this time.

"Just a little," she choked out.

"Then I'll be more gentle," he said. He opened his palm, which she had felt on the flat of her back or at her wrist or on her shoulders over the last week, and revealed two strings of tiny silver bells.

"Is this so you can hear me approaching when you and Cora are gossiping in the kitchen instead of working?" she asked. Jokes were good. Jokes distracted from thoughts that had nothing to do with Congress or the Cashmere and everything to do with how his hair would feel beneath her fingers. She wasn't one to miss an opportunity to take what she wanted, though...

She wobbled a bit, making sure not to overplay the quick jerky motion, then laid her hand on his head to steady herself. His hair was thick and silky and the warmth of his ear pressed into her hand; there was something strikingly intimate about feeling that delicate shell against her palm. She was about to pull her hand away, when she was distracted by the unintended consequence of her ruse. There was a jingle as his hand darted up and cupped behind her knee to steady her, but this touch was different from the light taps and corrective nudges of their lessons. It was his fingertips pressing into her skin through the thin material of her pants, his palm and digits exerting strength to grip and hold her in place.

Bertha swallowed hard and shut her eyes against the quick, sharp longing that lanced through her. He was completely still, unmoving save for a racing pulse where her palm met his ear. She couldn't tell if it was hers or his. Amir didn't move for a long moment, then released his grip on her. It wasn't a quick motion, but a slow caress that sent a tremor through her.

"You don't need bells to announce your presence," he finally said as he tied the string around her ankle. His voice was lower than it had been, the air around them a bit more charged, like the feeling in a room right before she launched into her dance.

Bertha was so focused on his touch and her response to it that, for a moment, she forgot what he was talking about.

His fingertips grazed the skin and bone of her ankle as he tied, each touch sending little shocks through her that marched steadily towards her apex like the soldier boys parading down Fifth Avenue.

His shoulders rose and fell on a sigh, then he looked up at her and grinned, and it wasn't until his dimples sank deeper—an indication of growing amusement—that she realized what he wanted. She switched the foot that rested on his knee and reminded herself that she was indifferent to his presence as he tied the second string. That his touch did absolutely nothing at all to her. He was just a man, and one in her employ at that.

"There," he said, standing. There was only the slightest

darkening across his cheekbones, and in his eyes, to show he'd felt even a fraction of what she had. "This is a bit of baiji—natchni, a form of the kathak we were already doing."

"Like nautch?" Her voice came out smooth, no breathiness, no husk. She couldn't let him see that he'd affected her any more than she had already revealed. Once a man knew he affected you, he started getting ideas, and in Bertha's experience those ideas were never good for her in the long run. Getting the Cashmere from Arthur had been a stroke of luck—cunningly executed, but luck all the same. She couldn't go all soft-headed over a man now.

"Yes. A version of nautch is what has been exported to Britain and the US." He had enough tact not to show his disdain.

She'd occasionally gone to nautch shows to pick up new techniques, when it was allowed; sitting in the Colored section of the theater as a White woman whirled to Indian music.

"Traditionally, a natchni would travel with her husband, or master, and dance and sing while he played. After the performance…" He looked away from her. "Nevermind."

Something about his expression pricked at her. She knew very well what happened after performances, no matter the country or culture. Men wanted what they had just seen, and if there was a "master" in the mix, he likely profited from that. Her father had never done so, and had gotten into brawls when admirers pushed their luck. Arthur had been a good egg, but he hadn't been possessive; men offering the right price had been able to indulge their fantasies of Bertha in nothing but her bangles.

You don't mind, do you? You know we got bills to pay...

"I'm going to clap, since we have no drum here," Amir continued, and Bertha shook away the thought. "For each clap, step firmly once so that you match it with a jingle."

He began clapping, looking at her expectantly, and irritation tugged at her like a rough john. She held up a hand, but not to dance.

"First answer this: in addition to people from the expanded Asiatic Barred Zone, what other group is no longer allowed entry into the US effective February fifth of this year?"

He cocked his head to the side, eyes turned up as if he searched for the question on her ceiling. "Apart from madmen, criminals, and any other bogeyman politicians could think of? Apart from people like me?" He met her gaze then. "Illiterate people. People over the age of sixteen must take a literacy test before being allowed entry. The same way Blacks in your Southern states are given tests before being allowed to vote."

Bertha raised her brows. "Very good. You're right, with the exception being that there's a chance of passing the test immigration gives foreigners, whereas the tests for Negro citizens are generally not passable."

He nodded, then worried his bottom lip a little like he did when he was turning something over in his mind. "Does it make you hate your country? Knowing such things happen and no one stops it?" He ran a hand through his hair and Bertha's fingers flexed. "I felt a kind of hate in my heart before I left home, and I thought it was for my country, for what the British had made it. Now I don't know."

Bertha had felt that churning, directionless rage. Every time her father forced her to straighten and curl her long hair because an Indian girl wouldn't have the naps that even her "good hair" didn't hide. Every time someone directed bile at her because they knew she was Negro, and every time they fawned over her because they fell for the lie that she wasn't. Every time she felt glad when she was allowed something that America generally kept from citizens like her because she had tricked others into thinking she was foreign.

Girl, people see what they want to see.

"I don't hate America." She resumed her position, arms raised. "If I hated it, that would be admitting they'd broken me. We can both clearly see that I'm not broken."

She stood with her back straight, and her gaze trained on the wall behind him. It was how she had stared into the back of the crowd before beginning her dance so she wouldn't have to see the anticipation for the whirling, spinning lies she was about to create.

She pursed her lips. "You said you were going to clap."

He let out an indulgent sigh and then bought his hands together hard. Bertha closed her eyes, listening to the jingle as she stepped her feet in time.

🙰 🙰 🙰

Later that evening, she swept through the club, knowing all eyes were on her. Her dress was scarlet and so were her lips. The dress was loose fitting but still managed to cling to her curves, and the hemline brushed well above her knees. Her hair was pulled back into a heavy bun; she looked longingly at the younger women with their chic short cuts that didn't require hours of straightening and pinning and curling and wondered how freeing it might be to simply walk into the salon and tell Nell to cut it all off.

She was dressed a bit more revealingly than she had since taking over the club; before, when she had been one of the girls smiling at patrons and hoping to hook one to take to a back room, Arthur had insisted she wear as little as possible.

"Show them thick thighs of yours," he'd say, grabbing and squeezing. She'd acted like she enjoyed his rough touch because there had been no other option and, hell—sometimes she hadn't been acting. He'd been the source of power and protection in her world, and if he took a cut of her earnings and felt entitled to her goods, her lot was still a sight better than most women in her position. And she had no regrets; eventually, Arthur had gone from pimp to husband. Then he had passed away. She'd slipped into widow's weeds and cried—that hadn't been an act either—then held out a will with had her name listed as inheritor while her eyes were still rimmed with red. The Cashmere was hers, and now the girls didn't have to offer their bodies to anyone they didn't see fit to.

She had reminded them of that earlier in the night. "We want the men to vote yes. But the rules still apply; don't degrade yourself, unless that's the kind of thing that gets you steamed up."

The club was bumping as she passed through; cigarette smoke swirled through the air like steam rising from a manhole in the dead of winter. The scent of food and cologne and sweat permeated the air as people danced; she spotted Janie grinding on a flustered looking White man she was fairly certain was a local union big wig. Wah Ming was sitting on the lap of a brother who had connections with the Tammany drive to recruit Negro voters to the Democrats. Her throaty laugh mixed with the dolorous trill of a trumpet as Bertha passed the group. As she was walking, a hand shot out and grabbed her by the waist, pulling her down onto a firm lap.

Her neck stiffened and she jumped up, whirling in the cloud of smoke and bourbon scent.

"Do that again and you'll lose a hand," she warned, then her stomach plummeted as she recognition hit her. The man seated with a smug smile on his face was that combination of brown skinned and light eyed that inflated a man's ego, and between his political victories and his prowess in the sack, Bertha grudgingly had to admit that he wasn't completely full of hot air.

"Oh ho!" Victor held his hands up. "Still off the market? I thought you might make an exception for an old friend after all this time."

His eyes roamed over her body, as if mentally comparing her with the younger version of herself from a few years back. He knew her body about as well as any man, so he'd be a fair judge.

"You pay for the company of all your friends?" she shot back, lifting a hand to her hip.

"I'm a politician, baby," he replied with a shrug and a smile, and Bertha had to laugh at that. She appreciated when a man was honest about his faults.

She'd liked Victor; his fixation on her had been exhilarating at a time. An older, sophisticated man who treated her like a lady instead of a whore—most of the time. Sometimes, after a few drinks, he'd wanted her to do things he'd deny in the light of day, but he'd been good to her. After Arthur had died, Victor had learned very quickly that Bertha had no use for a man's relative goodness once she had her own power. Politics had pulled Victor to Albany shortly after that, immersing him in the political theater outside of the city, and she hadn't seen him since.

"What are you doing back in town?" she asked.

"I have a meeting with some of the men running for office," he said. "Tammany is looking to shore up the Negro vote. There's hope of getting more of our own into office this year."

"Oh, I wouldn't know about such things since I'm not allowed a ballot," she replied blithely. Victor looked around, then stood up, motioning for her to follow him. He maneuvered through the crowd, taking them to a dimly lit alcove where there was a bit less noise.

"I heard about your little challenge to the men," he said, his straight teeth flashing bright as he grinned. "I'm disappointed I won't get to see you dance while I'm here. I miss that."

Bertha's throat went tight. She felt like she was back in her office, Arthur's office back then, immediately after his death. Victor was using the same cajoling tone he had then. *I can take care of you, baby. You really think you can just step into his shoes?*

"Well, you'll just have to come back to town once we get the vote," she said. "Nice seeing you, but I've got business to attend to."

His hand went to her wrist, and it was nothing like Amir's warm touch—the only male touch she was used to now, she realized. Victor's grasp was urgent, possessive.

"I can help you," he said. "I've got sway with the state's most prominent Negroes, and many of the Whites too."

She looked at him, unsure of what was expected of her. "I'm sure your parents are very proud," she said, then tugged at her wrist. His grip tightened. It wasn't menacing, but he was making clear that she was going to listen, whether she wanted to or not.

"I know you're not naive, Bertha. Stubborn, but not naive." He gave her wrist a quick tug, pulling her against him. She'd once pretended she enjoyed that, but she no longer had to pretend, and the discordance froze her for a moment. His mustache brushed her ear as he spoke, and she shivered.

"You want men to vote yes," he said. "I can *get* men to vote yes."

She should have been pleased, but she knew he wasn't offering out of the kindness of his heart.

"What do you want?" she asked.

"A private dance, like you used to give before you got too uppity for it," he said.

Ah. There it was, a hint of anger belying the suaveness of his tone. She was too good an actress, it seemed, or he was too gullible. She'd presented herself as a woman not available at a man's slightest whim, and that was somehow a personal affront. He didn't just want a dance—he wanted her on her knees again.

"I don't do private dances," she said. "I don't do private anything."

"I'm traveling all over right now talking to groups about the upcoming elections. I've been asked to write an editorial for the Union League, explaining whether I'm for or against women having the vote," he said. "They say that men listen to me, that I'm good at changing minds. It will be published in all the papers, be seen by every man of consequence."

Bertha felt ill. She felt ill like the first time she'd let a man use her mouth and she'd gagged and almost been sick on the floor. She'd learned what to do since then, which Victor knew all too well.

"So you want sex from me in exchange for your word that you'll convince a significant number of men to vote yes?" She hoped laying it out before him would make him see how insulting his offer was.

"You've sold yourself for less." He wasn't trying to be cruel, but her hand went to the wall to hold her up. Her back was still straight, though.

He wasn't wrong. She was asking her girls to use their wiles; what would that make her if she said no? Just another pimp.

"You know there are men out there already spreading the word. Du Bois and the other race men are willing to do the same—what's right—without asking for anything in return."

He shrugged. "I'm a politician, baby."

She didn't laugh this time.

Don't degrade yourself. But hadn't she told herself she'd do anything? Well.

"If that's the only way you can get your rocks off, sure thing. Write your little editorial, show me proof that men have responded to it, and I'll make you forget whether you're coming or going. Just like old times."

The words came out sultry, velvety smooth, how she'd reeled in her customers night after night when she worked the floor searching for johns. They'd never known when she was faking it because she was always faking it.

"Is there a problem, Miss Hines?"

She turned, this time tugging her wrist away. Amir stood behind them, brows drawn and scowl lines pulling at that mouth of his.

"Nothing I can't handle," she said. He didn't move though, just stood there looking at her as if he'd strip his shirt off and pummel Victor if she gave the word. As if he could protect her. Her eyes filled at the foolish earnestness of it all and she blinked away tears that had sprung up out of nowhere. "Thank you for checking."

Victor harumphed, looking at the dishtowel in Amir's hand. "You can go back to the kitchen, boy."

She whirled on him. "And you can go back to your table." She tilted her head toward his party, who were laughing and carrying on. "Scram."

"I always loved that temper of yours," he said as he backed away. "You'll hear from me soon."

She stared him down, even after his back was turned. Amir moved to stand next to her, but he didn't touch her. Had he seen the tears before she caught herself? No one was supposed to, most especially not him.

"Can you come to the kitchen for a moment?" His voice

was level, as if he hadn't witnessed anything, making her all the more sure that he had. "I want you to try something."

"I'm working," she said. Her voice was harsh, but not more so than necessary given what had just passed.

"Brilliant. This is work related."

His elbow bumped hers playfully as he turned, as if beckoning her to follow him, and she did. She couldn't go back onto the floor just yet; couldn't have Victor looking at her as if she were a prize he had already won.

She smelled it as soon as she walked into the kitchen: a rich, tangy spice that made her mouth water.

"Cora?" she asked. Cora knew her way around the kitchen, but if she'd been hiding a recipe that smelled this good from her, they were going to have to have words.

Cora was sitting with her feet propped up on an empty box and a bowl of steaming food in her lap, looking content. She shook her head as she finished chewing. "I was craving fish stew yesterday and Amir said he'd cook me some. I make some good fish stew, so I can say with authority that this is some good fish stew."

She tucked in again, a radiant smile on her face.

"Try some," he said, grabbing a bowl.

"Why do you need me to try it?" Bertha asked. She leaned back, eyeing the pot suspiciously.

He laughed. "Because you didn't eat before practice this afternoon and I don't think you ate after, and you're going to be on your feet all night," he said as he ladled up the stew. "I told you it was work related. Here."

She took the bowl from him, and a spoon, schooling her face into a mask of annoyance to hide that inside she felt soft as kitten fur. She often worked so hard that she forgot to eat, not realizing it until a drink went to her head too quickly or she collapsed into bed as the sun came up. How had he noticed?

She scooped up a fragrant spoonful and made a sound of pleasure when it touched her tongue. Tangy, hot-sweet, lush—it was delicious. She said nothing, scooping up spoon after spoonful until the bowl was empty. The stew was rich, but she felt lighter somehow having eaten it.

"Thank you." She handed him the bowl. He took it with a grin and moved to the sink. "You better watch your back, Cora," she teased.

"I can't see my toes, let alone my back, but I'll try," Cora said.

Bertha laughed and moved to head back out onto the floor. It wouldn't do to be gone too long, though as she heard Cora and Amir chat she wished she could stay and sit with them. But she was the boss, and that was how she liked it.

"Let me know if you need anything else," Amir called out as she was going through the door. She looked back at him and his grin was gone. There was tenseness in his shoulders and jaw that belied the easiness with which he'd led her into the kitchen. His gaze flicked toward the door and then back to her. "Anything."

She should have said something cutting to remind him that she was in charge and she'd never need his help. That was how she made it through each day; reminding others of who she was and where they stood in relation to that. But she sheathed the cutting jibe and simply nodded.

Because while she hadn't needed his help, the taste of his food and the slant of his frown served as a counterbalance as she sauntered onto the floor, helping to pull her shoulders back and her head high, the better to look down her nose as she passed Victor. He winked at her as she walked by. She ignored him.

The election needed to be over, and fast.

chapter six

"Practice again today, Pintu?" Fayaz asked as Amir pulled on his coat, a shabby thing left behind by the flatmate he'd replaced. The autumn had been on the warmer side, but cold winds and dropping temperatures had descended to remind him that another interminable New York winter awaited him. His walk to the Cashmere would leave him chilled if he didn't get a new jacket.

If you're there for that long. He couldn't very well work as a dishwasher forever, could he? If that was the case, he'd be better off returning home and tending to his land, like Sabiha Auntie begged him to in her letters. He'd been giving it more and more thought, especially as his savings grew. He would be a peasant back home, but a well-educated, well-traveled one. He could tell stories to his children about the time he lived in a city far away, like Raahil Chacha had with him. Unlike before, Amir wasn't able to conjure up an image of a doting wife. Instead, he thought of sitting on the couch beside Bertha as they did after each lesson, sipping *cha* and talking politics.

"They *practice* every day," Syed said, drawing an annoyed glance from Amir as he struggled with the buttons on his coat; the previous roommate had been a slimmer man than him.

Syed peeked up from the letter he'd received from his mother, updating him about his wife. "You'd think they were planning to take the stage with all this *practice*."

Amir rolled his eyes before slipping into his shoes and heading through the door. "Keep this talk up and you can get someone else to cook for Azim's wedding. *Khoda hafez*."

"Eh, don't be so sensitive, Pintu!" Fayaz called out as the door closed.

It was hard not to be sensitive. The mere mention of Bertha twisted something in him that should have been straight. She was his boss. That was it. But Syed was right.

Although he learned something new during each of their political talks and her lessons, Bertha had learned enough from him by now. It wasn't as if he was some grand master of the art form—she was a far better dancer than him. He simply had more technical knowledge by an accident of birth. Her dancing had been more than fine when he'd first seen it. It was better now, but who would really know apart from the two of them? But instead of decreasing the number of practices, they now met every day, even when she wasn't teaching her citizenship classes. She was surely getting *something* from the meetings if she kept scheduling them, but he didn't know what, and that was why any mention of her from his friends was no joking matter for him.

He knew what he was getting from their lessons, and it wasn't just the finer points of American politics. Amir had gone to the fire rooms that fueled the *Kandahar*, had felt the heat of the great coal-fed engine, but that was nothing compared to the way he felt as he stood behind her and watched her hips move. His focus should have been the tips of her fingers or the angle of her shoulders as they rose and fell—not that those weren't distracting, too—but Bertha had made up for a lack of actual knowledge by moving in a way designed to ensure the audience paid no attention to the finer details.

Amir had fancied a woman before. He'd dreamed about his neighbor Nazia for years before an arrangement was made and she had been married to a man from another village. Once he'd made it to Calcutta, there had been Nita, the widow who rented out rooms and occasionally took her tenants as lovers. After her was Piyali, the café owner's daughter who had smoked cigarettes, worn British-style trousers, and spoken of revolution as they lay sweaty and sated in her bed.

But he fancied Bertha in a different way. Yes, every time he repositioned her arm or ankle during their lessons he imagined what it would be like to touch her everywhere. To kiss and lick her everywhere. But he also fancied her intelligence, and her toughness, and how she was the first person he'd butted heads with who'd butted right back, and with a smile.

Her smile. He thought of the look of pleasure on her face when she'd tasted the stew he'd prepared and his chest clenched. It had felt right, seeing her smile like that and knowing he had been the cause.

The thought warmed him against the cool autumn wind that snuck up under his jacket. The tumult of excitement and joy and apprehension that roiled in him each time he approached the alley leading to the back door of the Cashmere began to build. Those feelings were abruptly cut short when he turned the corner to the alley and saw a White man standing there, smoking a cigarette. Alarm bells went off in his head, louder than the calls to prayer that echoed across Kalinga Bazaar.

He's just having a smoke, Amir told himself. *He's not here for you.* He resisted the urge to turn and run. The man had already seen him, and running would give him reason to pursue. Amir hated that he had to plot his next move like a criminal, simply because a few sahebs had gotten together and decided they didn't want his kind around.

He kept walking, against his will, ready to flee if the man reached for him.

The man leaned against the wall, taking another pull of his cigarette but leaving room for Amir to pass. He tried to remain calm, to act as if he was just your average, every day, legal American citizen reporting for work. His apprehension began to decrease as he passed the man and heard no sign of pursuit.

"Hey."

Amir froze, a preliminary before taking off at a sprint. Then the man continued.

"You know any clubs around here a guy could go to for a good time?"

Amir turned and looked at the man. He had a thin, drawn face, and eyes like he'd spent too long squinting into the sun. He didn't look very much like a man searching for a good time, but then again, Bertha had explained that many of the Whites came to the club to gawk and stare, to "see the Negro in his natural habitat," as she'd put it. He'd told her about the sahebs and their wives walking through the slums of Calcutta holding handkerchiefs to their noses as they looked about, like they were at a zoo exhibit.

Oh my, they eat with their hands!

Although the Cashmere catered to a mixed crowd, Amir wasn't the one who got to decide who was allowed and who wasn't. He also had the sinking feeling that the man was more interested in him than in the club. "No. Only Negro clubs around here, sir."

He cringed at how the honorific slipped out. Why should he call some White man lounging in an alley like an urchin "sir"? The only power that the man held over him was the color of his skin, but that was all that was necessary in America, it seemed. Back home, too, now.

"Negro, you say?" The man didn't hide his appraisal of Amir as he continued to squint at him, or his skepticism. "Huh."

I don't want to go back. The panicked thought came out of nowhere, a sudden truth that bowled him over with the weight of it. He missed his neighborhood, his land, his people. But if he left he would miss the busy Harlem streets and the confusion that was America. He would miss Bertha.

"That's too bad," the man said, then looked away. "I know men who pay good money to find out about places like that."

He took a lazy drag of his cigarette.

Amir said nothing more, just turned and continued on his path toward the Cashmere. He used the key Bertha had given him for the back door and pulled it open, not looking back. As he passed through, he peeked through the crack left between the door and the wall by the hinges it turned on. The man was looking right at the open door, then turned and walked out of the alley.

Amir released a breath and told himself it was just a coincidence. Wouldn't an immigration agent have arrested him without preamble? The man had just been looking for a good time, and he'd find someone else to help him achieve that goal. He pulled the door closed hard behind him, making sure it was locked.

"Amir?" Bertha's voice called out.

"Coming," he replied. He tried to leave his paranoid thoughts and his disgust at his reaction, at the door. He had enough real life worries, like reminding himself that a dance was just a dance and Bertha was well out of his league.

❧ ❧ ❧

Bertha was behind the bar, looking through her ledger. Amir was stocking glasses he'd brought out from the kitchen. They'd practiced for a bit, his non-encounter with the man in the alley causing him to lose his train of thought a few times, and then they'd sat and talked. It had been comfortable; her on the couch with her legs tucked up under her, Amir beside her. The length of a cushion had separated them, and though he'd just been nearly pressed against her as he'd instructed her, he wondered if he'd ever be able to cross that gap on the sofa. It may as well have been the distance from his sleeping quarters in the bowels of the Kandahar to the officers' quarters above.

Then they'd gone downstairs, and his opening duties had brought him out to the bar and hers had brought her into the kitchen. Neither of them acknowledged the fact that the bartender would have stocked the glassware when he arrived or that Cora preferred doing the kitchen inventory herself. They'd done the same the previous day, and the day before that. They were performing a different kind of dance now, seeking each other out and then retreating, but he wasn't sure she noticed. It could be that she just needed a friend; she had men after her all the time, and Amir wouldn't be one of them.

"What did men do for pleasure while out at sea?" she asked abruptly. She didn't look up from her book and continued making notes as she moved her pencil down the column.

Amir fumbled a glass and almost dropped it, catching it at the last moment. "Pardon?"

She glanced at him. "I'm just wondering. What do men do, stuck out in the middle of the ocean with no woman around for a thousand miles? I'm sure some of them have no need for a woman and do quite fine for themselves, but what of the others?"

"Is there anything in particular that prompted you to ask this?"

"It's just that you mentioned how long your journeys were when we spoke earlier. Every night, I see men acting like goddamned fools because there are women around that they might have sex with. I wondered what they do with that energy when there aren't."

Amir placed a highball glass down on the shelf, carefully, and tried not to think about the word "sex." Allah give him strength, he didn't need to think of that any more than he already did when it came to Bertha.

She looked at him innocently, but the very primness of her expression—brows raised, mouth a contemplative pout—tipped him off that she knew she was toying with him.

"It depends. The officers did…officer things, I suppose.

Sitting around, looking important while they smoked pipes." Her lips twitched at that. "With the lascars, some men prayed a lot more. Some kept themselves busy with work. Some were too tired to do much of anything. I imagine they thought about sex a lot, and…relieved themselves when the opportunity arose."

"And you?" she was looking at her book once more, but he could feel her attention directed toward him. "How did you pass the time?"

"When I wasn't cooking or helping around the ship, I read in my bunk," he said. "A lot."

"Mm-hmm."

He moved beside her to stock the water glasses and she turned and leaned on the bar, her body facing him.

"Do you still read a lot?" she asked, a smile on her lips. She was flirting with him, and even though he knew it was a rote act for her it still made his heart pound in his chest like waves smashing against the hull of a ship.

"I'm rather private about my reading habits," he said, leaning his hip against the bar to mirror her stance. "So I'll refrain from answering that."

"Mm-hmm." The same two-syllable sound, but this time it came out low, almost a purr. Amir leaned toward her, not thinking but following the pull of the hum in her tone.

A crash and a cry of pain from the kitchen made his

heart lurch in a different way, and had them both spinning and jogging toward the door.

"Cora?" Bertha called out as they entered, and then they saw her.

She was hunched over, hand gripping the edge of the counter hard. Shards of glass were scattered around her feet, but he had a sinking feeling that the liquid on the ground had another source.

"I think he got tired of kicking and wants to take the natural way out," she said. Sweat beaded at her hairline and she pressed her lips closed against another shout.

"I thought you weren't due for another month," Bertha said. Her body was tense, all trace of flirtatiousness gone. "You can't have the baby now."

Cora shot her an annoyed look. "Maybe you should tell him that."

Amir touched Bertha's arm.

"Can you go ring an ambulance?" she nodded and rushed back toward her office. He knew she must have been terribly frightened because she didn't push back against being given something resembling an order.

Amir grabbed a pot and filled it with water. He placed it on the stove top, flame high, and dropped the heavy shears Cora used for kitchen work inside. Just in case.

"Cora, I'm going to bring you out to the main room. We can have you lie in one of the booths until help arrives."

He placed an arm around her for support and she gripped his arm tightly. "Guess I won't get to try that aloo stuff you promised me," she said as they walked. She was trying to make light of things, but her voice shook and her eyes were bright with tears.

"I'll bring you some at the hospital. Surely it will be better than the food there."

She made a keening noise as they approached the closest booth. Amir pushed the table away and laid her down on the vinyl-covered seat.

"I don't think he's gonna wait," she said, eyes wide.

Amir's heart thumped hard. He was afraid, too—afraid for Cora and her baby—but he'd learned on the ship that in any given situation one person had to take charge, and this time it would be him.

He grinned. "That's right. He's a go-getter. He's not going to wait around for a bloody doctor to make his debut."

Cora tried to smile back, but faltered. "Back home, there was a woman who was the best at catchin' babies. They said Miss Junie was a hundred years old and had caught a thousand babies at least. Even if the baby came out blue and quiet she could breathe life into 'em." She closed her eyes and tears streamed down her face and into her hair as pain gripped her again. "I should have never left. I want Miss Junie. I want Darryl."

Amir felt the panic rising in her; the same that was in

him, but multiplied by all of Cora's incalculable hopes and dreams for her child.

"Cora, look at me." He heard the sound of Bertha's return but kept his gaze on Cora.

Cora opened her eyes.

"You don't know me so well, but you know Bertha. Do you think she would let anything happen to you and your baby in the Cashmere?"

Cora's chest rose and fell. "No. Not if she could help it."

"Exactly right. Nothing here happens without her say so."

He glanced up at Bertha then and didn't have to guess at how the call had gone. Her expression was pinched but she inhaled deeply and drew her shoulders back before striding over. "Of course not. And I say this baby is gonna be fine. He's gonna be perfect."

"Is the ambulance coming?" Cora asked.

She nodded, then shook her head, then nodded. "It might be a while. There was an accident with a car and a trolley. They said it would be best if we could bring her in. Said labor usually lasts for hours."

She walked over and knelt beside Cora.

"Do you think you can make it to the hospital?" she asked.

Cora shook her head in frustration. "I don't know. I don't know anything. This is my fi—AAAghh!" One hand gripped the wood running along top the booth and the other the cushion. "No. No, he's coming now."

"Shit. Shit." Bertha sat planted where she was.

Amir tried to catch her gaze. "Bertha."

She didn't move.

"Bertha, love." Her gaze finally flicked to him. "Can you please go get the hot water and the shears from off of the stove? And a stack of kitchen towels? And bring them here?"

She let out a shaky breath. "You sound like you know what you're doing."

"I've heard the story of my birth from my father enough times. There was a heavy rain and he was too scared to leave my mother alone so he had to deliver me himself." His father had always said it was his proudest achievement. It wasn't until after his father had passed that he'd realized that his father had meant him, Amir, more than the birth itself.

His stomach lurched at the enormity of what they were about to do, but then Cora cried out and there was no time for fear.

Bertha nodded, galvanized by having a task to achieve, and headed for the kitchen.

"I...have to check if the baby is coming," Amir said. "We can wait for Bertha to get back."

Cora laughed around a grunt. "Miss Bertha like to pass

out if she peeks under my skirt. Just look. I don't care as long as this baby comes out safe."

He checked, not quite certain what he was looking for but sure it wasn't there. "Not yet," he said, wishing his father had gone into a bit more detail about the logistics of his delivery.

Bertha returned with the requested items. After placing them on the table, she slid onto the bench so that Bertha's head was in her lap. She wiped at Cora's brow with a damp cloth, her face drawn with worry. Amir held Cora's hand as she breathed through contractions, and they both offered her encouragement.

"I'm gonna push," she said eventually. Her eyes were wide with fear but there was determination in her grip on his hand. Amir looked at Bertha and she shook her head, so he moved down between Cora's legs. He knew some people would think it shameful, but sordid thoughts were the last thing on his mind as the crown of the baby's head became visible. Amir just stared for a moment, unable to move as he realized that there was no going back. Cora and her baby were depending on him.

"Okay, breathe and push. I think," he finally said, trying to keep his voice calm.

"Yes, that's right," Bertha said, holding Cora's hand. "Breathe and push. Push and breathe."

He was sure she had no idea what she was talking about either, but Cora needed guidance and she was providing it.

It went on like that for who knows how long, Cora working, Bertha and Amir talking her through the pain. Finally—finally—the baby's head and shoulders pushed through and Amir grabbed and pulled, wrapping the slick bundle in a towel. There was silence in the club, and Amir gently patted the baby's back. It didn't react for a tense moment, then he felt the baby's chest expand against his wrist and a scream pierced the air.

"Yes!" he shouted, leaning forward to pass Cora the bundle. "Alhamdulillah."

Praise God.

He moved beside them, grabbing the shears. Tears streamed down his face, mixing with the sweat, and when he looked at Bertha she was wiping her eyes. He quickly cut the cord and tied it. His father had emphasized that, at least.

"It's a girl," Cora said, her voice hiccupping from her sobs.

"She's beautiful." Bertha wiped at her cheeks. She looked at the baby and her eyes filled again. Amir's heart was full of wonder and joy, surging in him like a river with no outlet, and he did the first thing that came to mind. He leaned in toward Bertha, and when her head swiveled in his direction he kissed her.

It wasn't a lustful kiss, simply a chaste press of mouth against mouth, but it hit him with a force that nearly stopped his lungs from working. Then Bertha leaned in closer, pressing harder as if she needed more from him. He gave it to her.

The kiss deepened to something sweet and rough, just for an instant, and then she pulled away. Her gaze snared his and she let out an exhilarated trill, as if they'd just crossed the finish line at a race.

That was it; they were sharing in a victory and nothing more. She looked back down at Cora, who was entranced with her little girl.

"I'm going to go hail a cab," Bertha said. "We should get you to the hospital."

"Darryl is at work," she said. "Over at Baker's." Her husband stocked shelves at a local market.

"I can go tell him to meet you," Amir said. "I just need to wash up. "He was wiping his hands with a towel, his gaze traveling between Bertha and Cora and the baby.

"Harlem Hospital," Bertha said, and he nodded.

He headed toward the water closet, the thrill of new life—and the feel of Bertha's mouth—suffusing him with an emotion that made him sure he was glowing like an electric light.

"I have a name for her," Cora called out after him, and he turned to her. "Amira. Sounds nice, huh? I think Darryl will like that. Amira."

She looked down at her child again.

"I'm partial to it," he said, his voice thick.

His hands shook as he washed them, and he stopped for a moment and gripped the edge of the sink as the terrifying wonder of all that had just passed fully struck him. Wonder wasn't the only thing he was feeling; Bertha's mouth had been warm, inviting, and he tried to push away the image that had lodged in his mind during their kiss and refused to budge. Bertha, sweat-damp and happy, holding a brown baby who had his eyes and her nose. Men weren't supposed to imagine such things, *na*? Daydreams of babies and happiness were as naive as believing the streets in America were paved with gold and all people were welcome with open arms.

Amir buried the flash of envy and jogged into the cold evening air to tell Darryl the good news.

chapter seven

"Wait, Cora had her baby in *this* booth?"

Janie and Wah Ming jumped out of the seat where they'd been lounging against one another with matching looks of disgust on their faces.

"Ya'll know you both came from your mama's nethers, right?" Eve asked.

"Well, Cora ain't my mama," Janie shot back, examining the back of her dress.

Wah Ming's face relaxed and she shrugged and settled back into the seat. "I've seen worse than childbirth happen in this booth, if we're being honest. I've done worse, too."

She winked.

Janie sighed and sat back down beside her.

Bertha waited for them to settle down. "As you all know, Amir has taken over the cooking temporarily."

"Why temporary? The man can cook!"

A burst of agreement broke out from the group.

"I thought he was handsome, but after eating that fried chicken he made last night, I'm wondering if he's got a wife back home or if I can lock that down," Janie said.

Wah Ming nudged her.

"What? I'll share my chicken with you," Janie said. "Maybe not the chicken. You can have some of the greens though."

Bertha felt the tickle of something unusual at the back of her neck. She didn't like the idea of the girls discussing Amir's matrimonial status or joking about changing it. She wasn't jealous, though. And she certainly wasn't thinking of how his mouth had felt against hers, or the happy shock that had gone through her when he kissed her. She hadn't felt that way since her first kiss; behind a venue in Gary, Indiana with a boy who had come to the show three nights in a row and presented her with flowers the second two.

She'd imagined Amir's mouth against hers many times—many, many times—but her fantasies had leaned toward what she knew of men. Amir grabbing her by the arm and backing her against a wall, or some other louche situation. That his actual kiss had been so sweet and full of joy ruined the illusion. She couldn't imagine that he'd kissed her driven by lust or some baser emotion. His mouth had been warm and firm and decisive, and he'd laughed against her lips like they had accomplished something together. She would've fallen into that kiss if Cora and Amira hadn't been there, in need of immediate help. She almost had anyway.

That was a problem.

"Does anyone have a real question?" she asked. "Unrelated to Cora's delivery?" *Or Amir?*

A girl named Lucie raised her hand. She was a quiet one, though she did well with the men who liked to hear themselves talk.

"Why does voting matter?" she asked. "I'm just thinking about how Du Bois and everyone got all hopped up over getting Wilson into the White House. Wilson talked a lot of stuff about making things better for us, about justice and kindness, and look! Things are worse than ever with him in office. More segregation. More injustice. Hell, forget Wilson; the suffragettes didn't even want us at that parade of theirs." Lucie caught her voice rising and sank down in her chair a bit, folding her hands in her lap. "It just seems like voting isn't as hot as we're making it out to be."

Bertha looked at the woman, at the way none of them were meeting her eyes now.

"I see it like this," she said. "One time, a long time ago, I met a john who talked so sweet. Looked rich. Smelled good. Came in here telling me I was the prettiest thing he'd ever seen, begging me to put it on him, all that nonsense." There was a ripple of knowing laughter among the girls. They'd heard it all before. "I thought he was swell. Classy. Let him convince me to go back to a room with him."

The laughter stopped.

"That man threw me on the bed and started trying to get crazy. Thought because he was paying for it, he could do whatever he wanted. But I screamed and the man running the hotel bust through the door and pulled him off of me."

Bertha looked at the girls, and knew many of them had been there before, too, and some hadn't been so lucky. "What I'm saying is, I bet on that man. I thought he was the best choice of the pickings that night. I thought he was gonna do right by me. And I was wrong. That didn't mean I didn't go back to work the next night. That didn't mean I never got fooled again. When you're trying to survive, sometimes you're gonna encounter liars. Politicians are the worst of them. But there are good ones too. You take your chances there like anywhere else in life because the only other option is giving up. That make sense?"

There were a few shaky head nods in the group. Bertha felt a bit shaky herself. Had Amir heard that? She wasn't ashamed, but she still wondered how he might react.

A movement at the front of the club caught her attention.

"The club isn't open yet," Bertha called out. She'd told the last girl in to lock the door behind her, but of course whoever it was had forgotten.

"Well, good, because I've got a headache and I'm not in the mood for that ragtime noise right now."

Bertha startled when the person came into view from behind a column. She already knew who it was from the accented voice, but when the fur coat swept into view she was certain. Miss Q. She hadn't seen the woman since that day at the suffrage meeting, and she'd only been into the club a few times over the last couple of years. Rumor had it that she was mobbed with suitors angling for a slice of her numbers kingdom, and she wasn't having it. She held court in her own lavish apartment, hosting the finest minds of Harlem, ranging from musicians to artists to businessmen.

A flurry of whispers erupted from the girls.

"You can all go now," Bertha said, already stepping down from the stage. Miss Q had made herself right at home in a booth, and looked at her with a bemused expression as she approached.

Bertha slid in beside her. "Can I get you a drink?"

"No. Though I hear this Hindu chef you've got in the kitchen is maybe worth venturing here late night for."

He's not Hindu.

Several people had commented on the food in the days since Amir had taken over. Cora had been no slouch, but Amir had taken her recipes and made them into his own, incorporating spice mixtures close to those of his home country into the familiar down-home food Cora excelled at. The man knew his way around a kitchen.

"You should come try it some time," Bertha said.

"Oh, I will. I don't have time now, though. My driver is waiting outside. I wanted to talk to you about these classes you've been having."

Bertha tried not to show her surprise. "You know about the classes?"

"Girl, I have number collectors running these streets every day. When they're done with their routes they come back to me. They hand me the money and the numbers, and they tell me things they hear along the way. I know most everything."

She gave a meaningful look around the club and then looked back at Bertha. "Everything."

Bertha's heart slowed and her palms went sweaty. Could she know? About the forged will? About what she had done to survive?

Miss Q smiled. "But I also know how to mind my business. That's the most important thing." She leaned back in her seat. "I like what I hear about you, and what I hear you doing with these girls, even before the classes started."

"I just treat them like they should be treated," Bertha said with a shrug. She was still trying to figure out Miss Q's angle. Was she there to threaten her? To force her way into the business? She knew Arthur had borrowed money from the woman once, but that had all been paid up before he passed, or so he had told her. He had been cheap, but not a welcher that she knew of.

The thought of losing the club made her head spin. The Cashmere was her life.

"You say that like it's normal." Miss Q pulled out a long thin cigarette and lit it, moving idly as if Bertha weren't on pins and needles waiting for her to get to her point.

She inhaled deeply, then exhaled. "You saw what happened at that suffragette meeting. People act like just because you ain't in church or washing some White child's ass that you don't amount to nothing. But there are a lot more people who don't count than do, if that's the case." She shrugged.

"Is there something you want?" The question was rude, but Bertha was on edge. If Miss Q even suspected what Bertha had done with Arthur's will, Bertha would be under someone's thumb, yet again. Everything in her rebelled at the idea.

Miss Q laughed. "I like you. Direct and to the point. I don't want anything really, except to add some girls to your class. Few of the street girls who work over by me. And some of the money counters."

Bertha waited, but Miss Q didn't talk further.

"That's it?"

"That's it. You have smarts to share. I have girls who need more smarts."

Bertha's life had been full of strange bargains lately: dance lessons with Amir, classes with her girls, and a piece of her soul with Victor. But those all had clear cut rules. Miss Q certainly must have wanted something else.

"I can take a few more," Bertha said carefully. "I've been feeding my girls though, and I can't offer that to everyone if the group gets too big."

It was the truth; she was a businesswoman, not a saint.

Miss Q nodded. "I'll pay for food and drink for 'em. You're doing work, and you should expect to get paid."

Bertha held out her hand and Miss Q shook it. "Let's keep things straight—I'm not going to be in debt to you for any of this," she said. "Don't expect that a month from now you can show up and suggest I open a craps room or give you a cut of anything."

She held Miss Q's gaze, preparing for the worst. Bertha respected the woman but, like most people with a lick of sense, she feared her. Miss Q regularly crushed ruthless men who tried to cut into her territory under her heel like insects; Bertha had no doubt the woman could make her life uncomfortable if she so chose.

Miss Q released her hand. "I wondered about how you got this place out from under Arthur. You don't take shit."

"Now I don't," Bertha admitted. The set of her shoulders relaxed the slightest bit. "One day I just couldn't stand another minute of it. Of being told what to do and how to do it and that I'd better do it with a smile."

Bertha had never admitted that to anyone—it was the kind of confession that raised questions she didn't want to answer—but something in the way Miss Q regarded her made her think she might know a thing or two about that particular feeling.

"And then old Arthur ended up dead and you ended up with the Cashmere, huh?" She let out a low laugh.

"I didn't kill him," Bertha said. "God and a bum ticker took care of that."

Miss Q exhaled, her lips pulled in a not quite smile. "We do what we have to in a world that tells us we don't deserve even a bit of power. But if you say you didn't, then that's none of my business."

"Tell your girls to be here at two on Monday," Bertha said.

Miss Q nodded and got up to leave. She walked away, her fur coat trailing behind her, then turned. "I know I just said I was good at minding my business, but…" She glanced toward the kitchen door. "What do you know about this Hindu fella?"

He's not…

Bertha's stomach flipped. She'd thought the crisis had passed, but it seemed Miss Q had waited to hit her with a doozie.

Bertha's back teeth gritted against each other. "You also just said you valued directness. Whatever you have to say, say it."

"One of my guys says he saw your guy talking with one of them cops that've been hanging around here trying to act like they don't stick out like a sore thumb. Same as the one who showed up in The Romper Room before they got shut down."

No. No no no. She thought of Amir's soft touch against her wrist, her ankle. Of the way his dimples deepened like pools of mirth when she told him stories, and his dark brows furrowed when she explained about the electoral process and the rights of citizenship.

"He wouldn't," she said. "There must be some misunderstanding."

"You of all people should know a man can and *would* do anything," Miss Q said with a delicate shrug. "My guy didn't hear anything, just mentioned what he saw to me. And now I'm mentioning it to you. That's it."

Bertha nodded. "I'll look into it. Two o'clock Monday then."

The sound of Miss Q's heels clicked in the silence of the club, followed by the sound of the door opening and closing. Bertha knew she should feel anger, but instead she felt a deep sadness that spread over her body. It weighed her down, like the kudzu that had clung to the trees in her childhood home, eventually toppling them when their weight grew too much to bear. If her life had taught her anything, it was that people always left and men weren't to be trusted. There was no reason the thought of Amir ratting on her should have been particularly hurtful, and yet...

She got up and walked to the kitchen. From inside she heard Amir singing as he worked, his voice so low it was almost a hum.

She girded herself and walked in.

He was at the stove, as he always was now, his shoulders marking the rhythm to which he matched his song. He stirred something that smelled like heaven, and then lifted the spoon, swiped a finger across, and stuck it into his mouth. His eyes closed as he savored it, teeth scraping over his bottom lip to catch the last traces of the sauce, and Bertha felt a raw wave of want go through her, like a ripple going over water, expanding toward the horizon.

"Is it really that good?" That was easier than asking if he had betrayed her.

His eyes fluttered open and seemed to darken as they settled on her. No, Miss Q had to be wrong; men were low down snakes, but Amir was no actor. He couldn't fake the way he looked at her, and he couldn't look at her like that and then run to the police.

He insinuated himself into your life so easily. He's closer to you than anyone. Bertha began to tally the time spent with Amir over the last few weeks: hours and hours. Talking, getting to know each other. Being set up?

No.

He walked over with that slightly bowlegged stride of his that should have been ridiculous but made him seem confident instead.

"Want to taste?" he asked. His voice was rough, not at all how it had been as he sang to himself.

She nodded and reached for the spoon, but he held it aloft. Bertha was slightly ashamed but a tight heat bloomed between her legs, and when he slicked his index finger over the curve of the spoon she swallowed hard.

He lowered his glistening finger toward her lips.

"Are you fooling?" she asked.

"No one touches my cooking tools but me," he said, thick brows raised. "Do you want a taste or not?"

Dammit, he knew she wouldn't resist a challenge; she doubted he knew that this was one he would regret.

"Okay," she said. She leaned forward and traced her tongue over his fingertip. The sauce was delicious, but not enough to justify what she did next. She gripped his wrist with both hands, flattening her tongue to give his finger a few strong licks, then sucked it into her mouth. Amir should have known that playing with her was a losing game.

Maybe he wants to lose.

"Bertha."

Her name was a plea for help, or for more. She glanced up at him as she sucked once, twice, three times, loving the way his lips parted and his eyes went dark and intense. She released the digit with a pop and he squeezed his eyes shut.

"You're right. It's quite good," she said, dropping his hand. "I'll put it on tonight's menu. Be a doll and write out the name and description for me."

He didn't say anything; his breath was coming out ragged and his pants were tented at the groin, an intriguing hint that almost tempted her to continue. Almost. But it also meant he wouldn't be thinking straight and now would be the best time to catch him unprepared.

"I need you to ask you something." Her voice was cool now, bordering on harsh. "Have you spoken to anyone about what goes on here at the club?"

His forehead wrinkled, and she hoped his confusion wasn't only at the abrupt subject change.

"Just my flatmates," he said. "It isn't every day one delivers a baby."

Was he playing dumb?

"And no one else? Has anyone approached you?"

His shoulders rose and fell. "There was a man in the alley the other day. I thought he was from immigration."

There was fear in his expression now, something Bertha hadn't seen before. She usually ignored the fact that he was not here legally, that he could be taken away and thrown on a ship at any moment. It seemed absurd, the thought of such a thing happening, but she knew as well as anyone that people always left. That knowledge didn't make her feel any better.

"Why didn't you say something to me?" she asked.

"Because I was ashamed," he said. He turned to the stove and went back to work, his gaze locked on the pan before him. "I nearly ran from that man. Why? Because I was afraid that he would put me on a ship and send me home. In that moment, I was not Amir the chef, or the sailor, or the dishwasher. I was an alien and a criminal, all because my skin is brown and I hail from Bengal."

Bertha knew that gut churning feeling, of being forced into shame not because of anything you did, but who you were.

"Just…things are tense right now. Be careful who you speak to," she said.

He nodded and kept stirring.

She reached out a hand toward him, rested it on his shoulder. "Amir—"

"What are you doing tomorrow during the day?" he asked abruptly.

"I have nothing planned," she said, then realized that was a lie. "Apart from our next lesson."

"I have something to do, so I can't come tomorrow."

"That's fine." Maybe she did need to be more careful with him. She shouldn't have felt such a childish sense of disappointment that he was canceling their unspoken plans. It was just as well; their lessons had become more tea and talking than dancing these days.

And the talking is what you will miss tomorrow.

"Since you have no plans, I can pick you up at ten."

"What for?" she asked.

"So you can put our lessons to the test," he said. He moved to the cutting board and began chopping a large onion.

"I said I wasn't dancing until women got the vote," she replied.

He stopped chopping and glanced at her. "This is a private event, not a show. The dancing will be optional, in fact. I just thought it would be nice to do something. Together."

"Oh."

Bertha was nonplussed. Doing something outside of the Cashmere made whatever it was between them more real. Like he was courting her. Bertha had never been courted before, really; men had taken her out on the town, but only because they were getting their money's worth.

"Fine," she said. "Now you get to prepping. We're expecting even more folks tonight, since people have been spreading the word about your cooking."

She headed for her office to do the day's administrative work and told herself that the funny feeling in her stomach was from Amir's food and not the fact that she'd just been asked on a date.

chapter eight

Bertha perched next to her office window, staring at her pocketwatch. She had debated going outside to wait, but hadn't wanted to stand out in the street. What was she supposed to say when neighbors asked what she was doing? That she was waiting for a man?

She had been so taken aback at being asked to go somewhere outside the comfortable confines of the Cashmere that she hadn't realize the ramifications of it. She had been publicly off the market since she'd taken over the club; it was part of her mystique. She wasn't quite sure how she felt about stepping out in public with a man again, and with Amir being that man.

She was good at lying, but not to herself. Not about something this dangerous. She desired Amir. When he wasn't around, she wished he was; when he was, she wished he was closer. And it was more than desire. When she was with him, she felt the same foolish flame of hope that had flickered during her years on the road and her first months in New York, when she thought she'd become a famous dancer, before being extinguished. She wasn't a cold woman, but she had gone a long time without that particular warmth. Then Amir had strode in, arrogant and rude, and then arrogant and sweet, and Bertha was fairly certain she was going to be burned however this shook out. That didn't stop her from wanting to step closer, to hold out her hands toward the dancing light.

A truck pulled up in front of the Cashmere and she stuck her watch in her pocket and squinted through the window. The truck had "Cohen's Deliveries" written across the side, but when the passenger door swung open, it was Amir who hopped out. He looked up at the window, as if sensing her presence.

"Hey!" He waved up at her and she felt a little shock go through her. The wind tousled his thick black hair, and a wide smile graced his face. Beneath his open jacket he wore a bright-hued, short-collared shirt that went down to his knees, with slim trousers poking out from beneath. He looked like a handsome prince come to rescue her from her tower. Bertha didn't need rescuing, but it was hard to turn it down when it showed up looking like that.

He waved again and her lips pursed. No matter how dashing he looked, he was still a man standing in the street calling for her like she was a doxy. Well, Bertha *was* a doxy, but no one treated her like one. Not anymore.

She raised the window and leaned over the sash.

"I'll be down in a moment," she said.

"Yes, come on!" He did a little dance while looking up at her, playful and flirtatious, and it moved her so much that she was tempted to slam the window shut and lock herself in her office.

That was when she noticed it from her peripheral vision; the way traffic slows when there might be an accident worth checking out. The street was packed with people strolling on a Saturday morning. Many of them had already swiveled their heads or stopped to see what was going on. She could already hear the gossip mill churning up a current stronger than in the East River. *The former whore and her foreign lover. Bossy Bertha finally beds down.*

She slammed the window down and adjusted her dress. If she didn't go, there would be even more talk.

People see what they want to see.

She locked up and headed out to the street, slowly sauntering toward Amir, who was leaning into the driver side window talking to the man she assumed was Syed.

"Miss Bertha Hines, nice to meet you," the man said cheerfully, but his smile faded into an expression of confusion as she ignored his hand stuck through the window, pushed Amir aside, gently, and pulled the door open.

"Pleasure to meet you, Syed. Please move over."

"But—"

"Bertha, what are you doing?" She didn't have to look at Amir; she knew his brow was furrowed and those frown lines were showing. She should have stayed in her office. She should have said no to begin with. The excitement that had woken her up early to prep and pamper herself faded, and she felt silly for thinking things could turn out any other way but bad.

"What am I doing?" she asked tightly. "I might ask the same of you, calling at the window like you were raised in a barn. Look around."

His gaze moved away from her, took in the clusters of pedestrians who had stopped to stare.

"So? People are looking. That's what people do." She could see the hurt, the anger, there, but it didn't matter.

She sighed. "People also talk. If it gets around that I'm getting hollered at and driven around by strange men, the respect I've worked so hard to build up will be gone, just like that."

How could he not understand that?

Amir's expression grew thunderous. "Strange men?"

"You know what I mean," she said.

"I know exactly what you mean, Miss Hines," he said, then turned and stalked off to the other side of the truck cab. Bertha shut her eyes, but didn't flinch at the slam of the door.

This was why she had sworn off men.

"Ready?"

When she opened her eyes, Syed had moved over and was patting the seat. She climbed up, allowing him to pull her inside when her skirt hampered her movement. Amir remained silent, facing resolutely forward.

Bertha pulled the door shut, waved at her neighbors and the others who had stopped to gawk.

"Look at you, Bertha," her neighbor Delphine called out.

"Never too late to learn to drive!" Bertha replied in a voice that was two parts cheer and one part sass. Delphine laughed. Bertha had created the story, and no one would doubt it now. Amir would forgive her, wouldn't he?

Would you forgive him?

Bertha's stomach flipped and her eyes stung. She turned to Syed and gave him her best smile. "I really don't know how to drive."

Amir hissed something in Bangla and Syed replied in a placating tone.

"We can do this. No worries." Syed showed her how to start the car and took over the pedal control, blushing furiously when his legs touched hers, as Bertha controlled the wheel. After a block and a half, they stopped and exchanged seats. Amir faced out the window, and Bertha supposed that she had been foolish to think stepping out with a man who wasn't paying could have gone otherwise.

They had a long afternoon ahead.

ख ख ख

Amir stalked about the kitchen of the hotel where the wedding was being held, growling orders at the men who had volunteered to help with the preparation of the buffet. It was a beautiful venue, the use of it a favor to the groom, who had worked there for a few years now. The kitchen was large and clean, with the nicest stove top he'd ever seen, but even that couldn't lighten his mood. Syed smoothed over Amir's rough orders with smiles and song, keeping the mood jovial as the men finished the preparation of the *walima* feast.

Bertha's theatrics shouldn't have surprised him, but they had, and that surprise had turned into a simmering anger that wouldn't leave him, like a too-hot chili whose burn lingers on the tongue. It wasn't just any anger; it was the foul, sullying rage that came with the humiliation of being reminded yet again that, here, he could not be seen as just Amir. He was a "strange man," as Bertha had put it. He was something to be ashamed of. And that she was the one who had reminded him…

Amir thought of the letter from Sabiha auntie that had been awaiting him the previous night. The one that was crinkled and stained, with half his name smudged off because the letter had been rained on at least once on its journey from Bengal to Harlem.

How are things over in New York? Last you wrote, things

were not so well. You didn't say it of course, but I know you well enough even if I have not seen you for some years. I ask because it is time for you to come home. When you left for a short while, your cousin agreed to manage your land, and when he married, I did what I could. But now my Khoka is going to be a father, and I am going to live with him and his wife to help with the baby. That leaves the problem of your land. I don't know what will happen if you don't return; the land of your father and grandfather will likely be lost. I've asked before but now it is no longer a question: you must come home. Don't you want to come back, find a wife, and settle down? Or will you wait until something breaks you as it did Raahil? You are stubborn, but you know what you must do.

The letter had kept him up all night, the tug of home and the possibility of a life in the States twisting him into knots. That and thoughts of Bertha, of the undeniable attraction between them, and the possibilities it held. Her civics lessons, and their talks, had made him think that perhaps there was a place for him in America. That once he knew how the system worked, he could begin to change it. And then he had pulled up with Syed and she had looked at him how a zamindar looks at peasants come to beg for a few days' leeway with their rent.

"Azim and Maria are arriving soon," Syed said as he settled beside Amir, his tone gentle instead of teasing. Amir swallowed the mean-spirited response that popped into his head. This was a wedding celebration and he needed to rid himself of any bad feelings—like anger, or jealousy—that could taint the auspiciousness of the day.

He nodded.

"Try not to take it personally, Pintu," Syed said clapping him on the shoulder.

"What other way is there to take it?" Amir asked in a low, annoyed voice.

Syed rolled his eyes. "*Boka*. Always getting so worked up. Have you even said anything to Miss Hines about your feelings for her?"

"There are no such feelings," Amir said stubbornly, then crossed his arms over his chest. "She should know how I feel."

"The same way you 'know' that she intended to insult you earlier today?" Syed asked. "And how she knew that you meant to take her down a notch by making a scene? *Ak daley dui pakhi*. You two are a perfect match, truly."

"You're supposed to be *my* friend," Amir growled.

"Yes, and it is a friend's job to offer guidance when your head is stuck in your behind," Syed said. "Perhaps instead of scowling your way through the rest of the day you could try talking. You do enough of it at the flat, keeping me up at all hours with your socialist clap trap."

Syed laughed and Amir couldn't resist cracking a smile.

"You always want to understand every little thing," Syed said. "I'm not as smart as you, but I am not confused by what is happening with you and Miss Hines. Think with your heart and not with your ego."

Syed removed the apron covering his suit and left the kitchen, but Amir dawdled. He was still angry, but then he remembered Bertha's expression as she had marched toward the truck. Her mouth had been tight, but her face a mask of relaxed superiority. It had been the same look she wore when he'd found that man holding her arm and speaking low to her in the corner of the club.

Nothing I can't handle, she'd said flippantly when he'd arrived, ready to defend her honor. Bertha didn't need defenders though; she did it well enough herself. And him showing up as he had, calling her out into the street, had given her a whole new set of things to defend herself against.

Bloody hell.

He stopped in the bathroom to clean up, realizing that he didn't know where Bertha was. He'd brought her to a strange place and abandoned her in a fit of pique. So much for showing her a good time.

She was easy to spot when he stepped into the hall, despite the bright fabrics that had been hung to bring life into the room that was normally sedate in shades of beige and brown. She was a beacon of forest green velvet, calling to him from across the crowded room. Her dress could be called modest in its cut and length, but the way it hinted at her curves without revealing too much of them was just as distracting. Amir wasn't the only one who thought so.

She was surrounded by a group of men, smiling and talking animatedly with them, as if she was catching up with old friends. Fayaz, Syed, and several of the lascars he'd met since jumping ship were amongst them; all seemed enraptured by whatever it was Bertha was saying. He'd thought she would be upset, but she seemed to be in good humor. She said something saucy—he could tell by the way just the right side of her mouth curved up—and the men around her laughed. She wasn't flirting, but she was certainly enjoying the attention.

Did you expect her to cry at your absence?

He walked over, expecting Bertha to acknowledge him and the group to part, but she continued talking and no one else appeared to notice him. He stood on the edge of the group feeling like he was the one who was a newcomer.

"They are here!" someone called out and the group broke up. Some of the men scrambled towards instruments that had been set up beside a dais. Amir approached her, feeling a tremor of apprehension that settled in his shoulders.

"All done setting up?" she asked politely. She wasn't cold, or rude, but her words still sprung up in front of him like a brick wall. There was no intimacy, nothing to indicate that they were anything other than co-workers. He didn't think she did it to punish him. He had put her in an untenable position then lashed out when she reacted accordingly; she was likely trying to make the best of things.

"I'm done in the kitchen. And I'm sorry," he said.

She reached out and tapped his shoulder. "There's nothing to be sorry for. I got to drive a truck and I've spent the last hour chatting with some nice men who told me all about how Azim and Maria met. Thank you for inviting me."

That was when Amir began to worry. Her tone, the cadence of her words, the calculated movements: she was playing a role. She was pushing him away, retreating behind her ability to laugh and smile and say just the right things. She was treating him like the girls at the Cashmere treated their johns, and she would only do that if he had treated her how johns treat their girls.

"Bertha." He reached out and took her hand. He'd never held her hand for longer than a brief touching of palms as they danced before. It was soft—surprising, given how hard she worked—and not much smaller than his. And it was shaking.

A man he had met at past religious gatherings came by and guided them to a table as the band began to play. They took their seats and the door opened, and a beautiful bride walked in. She wore a traditional Western white wedding dress, simple and lacey, but her veil was a long, rich rectangle of fabric from back home.

It wasn't until his hand tightened on Bertha's, and hers tightened in response, that he realized they were still holding each other. He wasn't sure what it meant, but if she was willing to allow it, he'd hang onto her for as long as he could.

chapter nine

Bertha now understood why the bride's veil was so long. It was draped over both bride and groom for this last portion of the ceremony, creating an intimate space for them even as they sat before a crowd of spectators. The groom held a small, ornate mirror in his palm.

"What do you see?" the man leading the ceremony asked. She wasn't sure if he really held any religious position or was simply stepping in, playing the role required of him in a place where so few of the comforts of home were available to men like Amir and his friends.

"I see my future," the groom replied in a voice strained by emotion.

He handed the mirror to the bride, and even through the thin fabric Bertha could see how their fingertips brushed and then lingered. The question was repeated.

"*Veo mi corazon*. I see my heart."

The groom leaned in and kissed her then, and there

were shouts of excitement and joy in the crowd, followed by applause.

Bertha finally pulled her hand away from Amir's to clap, each slap of skin jolting something inside of her. She wasn't one to get emotional at weddings; she hadn't even cried at her own to Arthur. In a way, it had been another business transaction. But seeing Azim and Maria had ushered her into a corridor lined with possibilities she hadn't thought within her reach, possibilities that beckoned her to throw caution to the wind and explore them. The feel of Amir's warm hand in hers had beckoned as well.

"That was lovely," she said as the band picked up again. The guests, mostly men dressed similarly to Amir and Syed, got up, some to dance and some to help set up the buffet of delicious smelling food. "Thank you for inviting me."

"I'm glad you came," he said. He placed his elbows on the table and folded his hands together. Then that dark gaze, the one she'd avoided since he'd stepped into the banquet hall, had her in its grip. "Even if I didn't behave like it after you got into the truck."

"I apologize for hurting you," Bertha said with a blithe smile, throwing his words from that first day he'd come into her office back at him. She couldn't resist the reminder that this wasn't the first time he'd had something to apologize for.

"I'm just grateful you know you have the power to," he replied. His tone was low and urgent. "More than anyone."

Bertha's breath caught, and the mask she had donned during their silent truck ride began to crumble at the edges, to lift away and reveal the emotions swirling beneath. She couldn't have that.

"Excuse me." She stood and bustled away from the table, sliding through clusters of men lined up to congratulate the newlyweds and those heading for the food. She stumbled into the hallway and entered the first door she saw through a haze of tears warming her eyes.

Why?

Bertha knew she had power over men, one that had resided in her swaying hips and her clenching pussy and now rested on her denial of them. But she also knew that wasn't what Amir was talking about. She didn't want to think of what it was that drew him to her, or vice versa, because it frightened her. She'd never wanted a man for anything other than his power and Amir had none: not wealth or political capital or street cred. That didn't stop her from daydreaming about their kiss, or from feeling an odd emptiness in her apartment when she stumbled in after closing up the Cashmere and he wasn't there.

Foolishness. She had more important things to think of. *The vote. The vice squad.*

Neither of those things had driven her running into strange rooms on the verge of tears, though.

There was the *click* sound of the knob turning, then the door opened slowly.

"Were you in desperate need of a tablecloth?"

Bertha looked around and realized she had hidden in a linen closet. "I wouldn't say desperate, but I thought I'd stick my head in and see what kind of linens a quality establishment uses." She rubbed her hand over a pile of whites stacked beside her. "Very luxurious."

"I'm sure they wouldn't notice if you borrowed a few," he said. He tugged on a small chain hanging from the ceiling, illuminating the space, then shut the door behind him and leaned back against it.

A tremor passed over her skin, raising the tiny hairs, as she took in the tilt of his head and the jut of his hips as he leaned.

"Neither of us can afford to be arrested for theft," she said. She was still stroking the tablecloths because she didn't know what to do with her hands. Well, she knew what she *wanted* to do with them: cup Amir's face, run her hands over that broad chest, slide her fingers up the nape of his neck and into his hair. When she wanted something, she generally took it, but she wasn't sure how to take this, or even what *this* was. It was more than desire, more than wantonness, though she very much wanted to be wanton.

Amir kept his eyes on her. "I'm guessing you didn't run in here because you hate me, but now I'm going to ask because I think we need to make some things clear. Do you hate me?"

"You wouldn't have made it over that threshold if I

hated you," she said, rolling her eyes.

He pushed off of the door and took a step forward. "Well, perhaps you fancy me then?"

"I think you skipped a few rungs on the emotional ladder," she replied.

He came toward her then and didn't stop until he was nearly up against her. His hand rested on top of hers to stop her nervous petting of the linen. In the silence, the music from the band filtered into the closet.

"I invited you here to dance," he said in a low voice. "Do you want to go back out there?"

"Will it upset you if I say no?" she whispered.

"Only if you say no to this, too." He raised his arms, moving them in time to the music. He continued his dance, expression patient, and she realized that during all of their lessons they had never truly danced together. He'd shown her a move and she had repeated it for him, but they had never moved as one. She extended her arms, taking her position, and he smiled.

They didn't have their full range of motion in the small space; arms brushed as they rose and fell; shoulders knocked as they turned, and when she finished her spin facing away from him it was natural when her backside brushed against his groin. They swayed like that as the song ended, and didn't resume their starting positions when the next song began. Instead, his hand went to her arm and turned her so she was facing him.

"I know a man fancying you is nothing new but—" he dipped his head so she couldn't see his eyes "—I do. Quite a lot."

She'd seen Amir when he let his quick temper get the best of him; they'd gone toe to toe more than once. But that head dip, and the hesitancy in his voice, told her more than his words had.

"Amir?"

His head lifted and his gaze clashed with hers. She didn't even have to say the words that were on the tip of her tongue before he was following through on them. His head dipped again, but not in uncertainty this time. His decisiveness had returned, and there was no hesitation as his mouth covered hers. This kiss wasn't sweet, like the one they'd previously shared, despite the fact that he tasted of spiced honey. His lips were firm and demanding, and when he slid a hand up the back of her neck to hold her in place, heat raced through Bertha's body.

The spark she'd felt during their celebratory kiss hadn't been a one-off. Her body was humming from his touch, and she wanted it to sing. She slid her hands around his waist and flattened her palms against his back, feeling his muscles tense under her touch through the fabric of his shirt. She took his bottom lip between her teeth as she moved her hands, worried it a bit, but then his grip on her tightened and his tongue pressed into her mouth and Bertha moaned with pleasure.

They kissed until her lips felt raw and bruised, hands running over each other's bodies. She could feel his hardness pressing against her, and she forced her hand between them, down low so she could stroke his length through his pants. It had been too long since she felt this rush of emotion: fear, pleasure, curiosity, and desire, all tumbling around in her belly, creating an ache that only Amir could soothe.

His hands slid to the front of her dress and Bertha felt the release of pressure as he undid the buttons holding the fabric tight against her breasts. Then there was a different kind of pressure as his fingers found her nipples, teasing them as his mouth passed rough-gentle over hers, only moving away in the brief instances when he needed to breathe.

Bertha had never been what people would consider impulsive—her life had been committed to weighing and measuring what she could get away with for as long as she could remember—but it seemed Amir had changed that. She began gathering the material of her skirt, lifting, with one mad idea in mind. It seemed the madness had gripped Amir as well because he was raising his long suit shirt. She pulled one hand away from her skirt to run her hand over the furred ridges of his stomach and the waistband of his pants. Her fingertips delved into the waistband, then his hand clamped around her wrist.

"Look at me," he said, and for a second she wished she had disobeyed him because his eyes revealed everything. Adoration and adulation, tinged with something darker and deeper. "I've screwed for fun before. This isn't fun, if we do this." A bit of the seriousness left his face then, replaced with a cocky grin. "Not just fun, that is."

She slipped her hand into his pants completely, circling thumb and forefinger around his girth. "I've screwed for profit before, and I have to say I think we'll both profit from this. We'll have fun, too. But there's not *just* anything between us." She squeezed him tighter, stroked, perhaps to distract from the fact that she was going to reveal something of herself. "There hasn't been since you walked into my kitchen."

He thrust up into her hand and at the same time pulled her into a kiss, and after that there was no more talking. His hands moved down to grip her thighs and his thumbs stroked rough circles against her sex. She pumped her fist around him with short, tight jerks. When they were both panting and muffling groans, he turned and bent her over the stack of tablecloths. The sweet pleasure of him pushing into her was tempered with the briefest flash of doubt.

Not like this.

Then he stopped, suddenly leaving her empty.

"I want to see you," he panted, switching places with her so he was sitting back on the linens. She lowered herself onto him, watching his pleasure at her clench express itself in the arch of his brow, and the way his eyes slammed shut and then opened. For a moment, she exaggerated her pleasure, threw her head back and bit her lip; habit was hard to break. Amir leaned up and kissed her again, then rested his forehead against hers as she rode him.

"I want to see *you*," he groaned. His hands cupped her face, stroked her neck and clavicles, as he pumped up to meet her downstroke, but his gaze never left hers. Heat built in her as he watched her, and annoyance.

What did he want?

But he'd just told her.

She placed her hands on his shoulders and instead of meeting his gaze in challenge, she simply watched him. She didn't fake a damn thing, just moved, and then she felt it. It was as if something in the way Amir watched her, and held her, allowed her to feel her passion in a new way. Each stroke within reverberated through her body. The soft brushes and hard squeezes of his fingertips drove her closer to the edge. Even the friction of her bunched dress against her skin sent tremors through her. And when he began pumping wildly into her, eyes still locked on hers, Bertha bit back a scream as ecstasy filled up every bit of her and searched for release. She turned her head and bit down on the meat of his hand as her climax took her, and then he arched into her, surrendering to his own.

As Bertha drifted down from her bliss, she could hear the music in the background once more, reminding her of where they were. She touched his face gently, and he kissed her fingertip.

Yes, this Amir was going to be a problem.

chapter ten

Amir lay back on the couch in Bertha's apartment, watching her as she dressed for the pre-Election Day party. The blood was only just starting to flow back into his brain; he'd been the one to pull her down onto the couch, but she had rendered him useless when she crawled onto his lap. The week since Azim's wedding had been a blissful blur. Bertha and her girls handing out suffrage pamphlets to men in the streets of Harlem. Amir bringing in Syed to be his line chef during the busier dinner hours as the number of guests exploded. And every free moment that hadn't been devoted to the vote or to the club, they'd spent with each other: touching, tasting, mapping each other's bodies with fingertips and tongues.

It seemed they couldn't get enough of each other. Amir had even started to spend the night, after making a show of leaving if anyone else was around, of course. Now he knew that she tossed and turned in her sleep, as if all the brisk energy that carried her through the Cashmere still flowed through her even when she tried to rest. He knew the taste of her in the morning, evening, and afternoon.

Nothing else mattered when he was with her, which was a dangerous thing. Another letter had come from his aunt about his land, and he would have to make a decision that didn't involve choosing between Bertha's soft lips and softer thighs. That didn't involve her sharp wit and the way he felt an actual pain in his heart, like he'd eaten too much *jhal-lanka*, every time he looked at her.

"Can you zip me up, baby?" she asked, looking back over her shoulder and Amir felt something that was startlingly close to anger. Not at her, but at even the possibility that he would have to leave her. He missed home—sometime the ache caught him unawares, triggered by the most ridiculous things—but thinking of a life without her sharp words and soft smiles singed like a hot pan that he had taken in his hand and couldn't let go of.

He lifted himself from the couch and moved to her, sliding his hand into the back of her dress and splaying it over her skin.

He looked at her face in the mirror and took in their reflection. Her eyes were closed and a gentle smile tugged at her lips. This was his Bertha, the one he was sure no one saw but him. It did something to him, to know that some part of her was reserved just for him. He hoped she knew that it was the same for him; though they still butted heads over some things, he also backed down instead of pushing, a feat his family had never thought could be achieved. He told her his hopes and his fears, though not all of his dreams for his future. Possibly *their* future. He was impulsive, but knew that telling her the idea he'd been mulling over would be pushing her too fast. If she didn't feel the same way...

"I wish I could stay like this sometimes," she said, voice low. "The way I am when I'm with you."

"Like what, love?" he asked.

"Like...myself," she said in a soft tone. Then shook her head and opened her eyes. "Tonight's a big night. Zip?"

And just like that, his Bertha was gone and Bertha the boss was back. He hoped that version of her was his, too, but he couldn't claim either version until he had decided what to do about his land.

"Are you nervous?" he asked as he zipped. "About tomorrow?"

"I just want the election to be over with," she said, giving herself a final glance. "I was silly enough to let myself start getting hopeful, and that never leads anywhere good."

It didn't take a leap of imagination to conclude she was talking about more than voting.

"What about you?" she asked, shifting the subject away from herself. "How will you feel tomorrow if I can vote and you can't?"

He knew why she had to ask; the very first time he'd heard about the suffragettes his reflexive response had been a resentment that surprised him. He'd considered himself more evolved than most men, had worked side by side with women in his political groups back home, and his instinct had still been to think that his own interests should be addressed first. "Well, I guess I'll have to get better at our political debates and try to win you over to the socialists."

She smiled and kissed him on the cheek. "I do look good in red," she murmured before swaying out the door. Amir followed. He couldn't argue with that.

They headed down into the club and as soon as they stepped on the floor business tugged them apart. There were glances and the occasional touch, but Amir was sweating in the kitchen with Syed, chopping and prepping, frying and sautéing. She was on the floor, managing the girls, the bar, the bands, the stage, and the surge of people who had shown up for the special event.

Once he got into the zone in the kitchen, there was nothing but the orders and fulfilling them, making sure each plate was perfect because this night was important to Bertha and she was the most important thing. Hours went by and eventually the orders started to slow.

Amir took a drink out of a pitcher of ice water, used a kitchen towel to wipe his brow. Syed dropped onto a stack of milkcrates.

"I hope that was the last of it," he said. "I can't even see straight right now, Pintu."

The doors swung open and Bertha strode in. She flopped onto a chair beside Syed. He'd known things were busy out on the floor, given the number of orders that had rolled in, but it was the first time Amir had ever seen her sit on the job.

"I'm starting to wonder if you're sprinkling something extra in the food," she said. "Or if it's just election fever."

"Maybe a bit of both," Amir said.

"Modesty doesn't suit you," she said. She was looking at him with that heat in her eyes, despite her fatigue, and for a moment he wished they were alone.

"Maybe going back home won't be so bad," Syed said, scratching his side. "You can open a restaurant and make your Bengali American food. You'll be the star chef of Calcutta by next year."

Bertha had been slack in the chair, but Amir saw the moment her neck went stiff and her mouth went tight. She eased her way up as the slouch left her back.

"You have plans to go back to Bengal?" Her voice was casual, in the way a shard of ice could casually slide off of a sloped roof and slice you open.

Amir's throat tightened. He hadn't known how to tell her about the letters; all the talking they did and he'd managed to avoid bringing it up. If he didn't go back, she had no need to know, and if he did…

"There's a problem with my land and I might have to go back," he said with a shrug. "It hasn't been decided."

"It hasn't been decided? Is someone else making the decision for you?"

He tensed at her tone. "Look, I'm trying to figure this out. It's not your problem, so don't worry about it."

He knew it was the wrong thing to say as soon as the words left his mouth.

She stood up and adjusted her dress. "I guess I won't then."

Amir bit back against the frustration building in him. "Bertha wait—"

"For what? People leave. It's what they do." Her expression was hard but her eyes were glossy; he had hurt her. Again. "I'm needed back on the floor."

She swept out of the room and he whirled on Syed, who held up his hands.

"Don't get mad at me, Pintu. You've been practically living with her for the last week. If you didn't tell her, I'm not the one you should be mad at."

Amir growled and threw his towel across the kitchen; it landed in a bucket of dirty water. Frustration pulsed through his veins. "I meant to tell her. I just hadn't decided what to do."

Syed raised his brows.

"What?" Amir snapped.

Syed raised his brows higher. "You know I have a wife at home," he said. "When I got on the boat and when I hopped off the boat, it was both of our decisions. You wanted this lady to bloody fancy you and once she does you pull something like this."

Syed shook his head and Amir knew what he was thinking.

Always making a mess of things.

He had messed up. Again. And he didn't know how to fix it this time. He hadn't just kept something from her, he'd kept the biggest thing from her. He hadn't wanted to admit the truth to her because he could hardly admit it to himself.

I don't want to go back.

How could he tell someone that his homeland no longer felt like home? That the only place he wanted to be was at the side of a woman who had no use for him in a country that didn't want his kind? He'd always thought he would go back and change things for his people; what kind of man did it make him if he didn't? And how could he have told her about the letter without heaping unspoken pressure on their new relationship?

"I'm going to talk her," he said.

Syed nodded. "Go on. I'll come get you if an order comes in."

Amir walked out into the club, which was busier than he'd ever seen it, though it was very late. A man sat at the piano, his fingers flowing over the keys so quickly Amir could hardly see them. A woman at the mic sang a suffragette anthem in a husky voice, jazz style, and the crowd nodded along. He scanned the smoky room and didn't see Bertha anywhere, so he made his way into the hallway towards her office.

He sensed she wasn't alone before he turned toward the already open door. Bertha sat on the edge of her desk, her crossed legs exposing smooth skin all the way to her upper thigh—exposed, save for the hand that rested on her knee.

The man who'd had Bertha in the corner that night that seemed so long ago sat comfortably in a chair, his fingertips caressing her knee until he followed her gaze and saw Amir.

"Can I help you, Amir?" she asked. Her face was perfectly composed as she lifted the man's hand away.

"I wanted to talk to you," he said, trying to remain calm. He'd already driven her away with his words, and if he couldn't contain himself he would lose her for good. Even a stubborn ram exercised caution when it met a worthy opponent.

"Well, as you can see, I'm busy." She flashed her saucy smile, but her eyes were shuttered, dousing the effect.

"I don't mean to insist, but I think it's rather important." He didn't have to try to keep his voice calm anymore, because he was so beyond anger and despair that he seemed to be operating on another plane. His hands hung limp at his sides; he couldn't even manage a fist. He felt disconnected from his body, disconnected from the possibility that Bertha had already written him off, and that he'd managed to plummet from *Jannah* to *Jahannam* so quickly.

"Oh, so now it's important." She nodded, several tight jerks of her head, but he knew it wasn't because she agreed with him.

"Get in line, buddy," the man beside her said. He

touched Bertha's knee again, like he had the right to. "There's enough to go around, if the price is right."

Bertha started saying something to the man, but Amir didn't hear it because his numbness had lifted and anger rushed into him, pushing him toward the man in three quick steps. It didn't matter if he'd already lost her, or even if she had chosen this man over him. He grabbed the man by the lapels of his fine jacket.

"Apologize to her. Now."

"For what?" the man asked. He wasn't afraid, and in fact seemed to find the situation amusing, if anything. His gaze went back and forth between the two of them and then he let out an abrupt laugh. "Ohhhhhhhh, I see. This is why you're trying to renege on our bargain. You're his woman now?"

What bargain?

It didn't matter. Amir gave the man a shake. "Bertha is her own woman."

The man laughed again, then pried Amir's hands away more easily than Amir would have imagined.

"You got a funny way of showing that," he said, straightening his shirt. "Shit, Bertha, never would have pegged you for that kind of sister, but I don't need to force a woman. I'll call in this debt some other way."

"What debt?" Amir was angry and confused but neither of them acknowledged him.

"You'll be repaid with my vote, if I get it—and if you earn it," she said, then inclined her head toward the door. "Beat it, Victor."

The man chuckled ruefully as he walked out. "Good luck, buddy."

"Are you going to explain what just happened?" Amir asked.

"No." She walked around the desk and sat down. "You're leaving, right? So it doesn't matter. None of what happened matters."

The words were forced, as if she were telling herself at the same time she was telling him.

"I don't know if I'm leaving," he said carefully.

"Well, you didn't think it important enough to tell me either way, so the point still stands."

"Not important?" Amir ran his hands through his hair in frustration. "This is the most important thing, Bertha."

You are.

He walked over to her desk and turned her chair so that she was facing him. He couldn't talk about this with her desk between them, the way they discussed food deliveries and the nightly menu.

"How was I supposed to tell you why I might have to go back to Bengal without explaining all the reasons I cannot?"

She looked down, refusing to meet his eyes, so he dropped to his knees and looked up at her.

"What was I supposed to say? 'Oh, by the way, even though I'm here illegally and can't get a well-paying job or even my citizenship, I think I'm going to give up my family land because I'm in love with you and want to stay here'?"

Her eyes widened. "What?"

"You can't even be seen in the street with me without feeling compromised and I'm supposed to put the pressure of my future on you? I couldn't do it without feeling like I was forcing your hand, and I didn't want to be just another man trying to make you his," he said. "I was wrong, and I made a mistake, but not because you aren't important. If you don't believe anything else, please believe that."

Her hand went to his face, and he closed his eyes as her fingertips brushed against his stubbled cheeks.

"Maybe I'm too good at this acting thing," she said softly. "If you thought I wouldn't want to hear that."

Relief rushed through Amir. He hadn't meant to tell her *that*, but he had and she hadn't spurned him.

"I'm sorry," he said again.

"Don't think you're getting off that easy. I'm still mad enough to spit nails," she said. "I felt like my legs got knocked out from under me, and I don't handle that well."

"I know," Amir said, turning his head to kiss her palm. "I'm the same way. You may have noticed."

She sighed. "Looks like we're gonna have a bumpy road ahead."

"I'm a village boy. I'm used to bumpy roads."

She laughed, not too loud but it seemed like it, and that's when Amir realized the music had suddenly stopped.

"What—"

There was a commotion in the club and it wasn't because someone was blowing hot on the stage. Bertha jumped up and peeked through the curtains.

"Shit."

A chill went down Amir's spine as she whirled away from the window, and the sound of falling chairs and the scrambling patrons reached him at the same time. She was boss Bertha again, and she snatched his sleeve and pulled him to his feet as she marched toward the door.

"Cops are here," she said. In the hallway, the sound of people screaming and glass crashing could be heard more clearly. Instead of heading toward the noise, she pulled him in the opposite direction, toward her apartment door. She turned the key and pushed him into the hallway that led away from the club. "Go up to the apartment. If they try to get in through this door, go out the front door and head up to the roof, then cross over to one of the connected buildings."

Amir wasn't quite comprehending what she was saying or how she could say it so calmly.

"What? What about you?"

"This is my club and the girls are my responsibility. Now go."

"I can't—"

"You can't do anything down here but get in the way and get your ass hauled onto a slow boat to India. If you meant anything you just told me, you'll go. Now."

He wanted to argue, to butt heads, but instead he pulled her into a kiss. It was brief, but he put every bit of his love into it. And when she pulled away and ran into the fray, he locked the door, went up to the apartment, and did the only thing he could. He knelt and he prayed, hoping Allah was truly as flexible as Amir believed Him to be. If not, he might lose Bertha for the second time that night.

chapter eleven

"This isn't quite how I imagined I'd be spending Election Day," Bertha said, examining her nails instead of the décor in the sterile office she had been marched to. Her eyes were gritty from lack of sleep—the jail cell hadn't been the most comfortable place she'd spent a night, but not the least either. Worries about her girls, her club, and, most of all, whether Amir had been taken had kept her up, staring at the ceiling of the dank jail cell until daylight had begun to filter in through the barred windows. She was exhausted and scared, but she couldn't let the man across the table know that.

He pulled out a file and opened it, calmly flipping through the thick stack of papers. He had such a benign face, like a white-haired grocer you forgot as soon as he handed you your change, but Bertha wouldn't be put at ease by it. Gregory Barton was the head of the Commission of Fourteen, meaning he had taken up the mantle of purifying the city of whores, drugs, and race mixing. That he even saw the latter as a vice didn't bode well for her.

"Miss Hines, your establishment has been a hotbed of immoral activity for some time. Lewd dancing. Women selling their bodies. It says here that the act of fellatio was observed more than once, carried out in bathrooms and alcoves."

"Oh dear. Is that so?" She raised a hand to her mouth and widened her eyes. She wondered who had relayed this information, mentally running through a list of regular patrons in her mind, but it could have been anyone. She knew that the commission paid well, and not everyone who came into the club was in a position to turn that down.

Barton glanced up from the file. "Don't get cute, Miss Hines."

"Well, I can't help it, sir. I was born this way." She batted her lashes, though she was sure her make-up was a mess. The urge to be sick pushed at her throat. She could not, would not, let him see that.

He didn't smile, but he didn't frown either, and Bertha counted that ambivalence as a win. Some people would be groveling or lashing out, but she was trying to toe the line that led to her getting out of jail with her body, soul, and business intact.

"Patrons of different races were allowed to co-mingle." He looked up at her.

"My club is strictly Negro, sir. If anyone else got in, I wouldn't know, as I'm color blind." More lash batting.

"And on top of all these offenses, you personally spearheaded a push to influence male voters in your establishment on the issue of suffrage."

Bertha tilted her head to the side, unable to hide her surprise at that. "Is voting a vice, sir? If that's the case, I can direct you to several locations where men are brazenly engaging in that very act today."

Barton dropped the file to his desk, the wrinkles on his brow deepening. "It's undignified behavior for a woman. And for your kind, it's unseemly."

She hoped that the men heading out to the polls were more enlightened than the one before her. She hoped Amir was somewhere warm and safe, not being detained in a place certain to be more frightening than the bland office she was in. She wouldn't know the status of either hope unless she was released. Inside, she was fuming, ready to flip the desk over and make a run for it, but she couldn't show that. She would play this cute and flirty; if she kept things light even in face of his ignorance she might have a chance.

"I know what's unseemly—not getting to choose who represents me as a citizen, or who fills well-paying positions like the one you currently occupy."

Well so much for playing it light.

The man's lip curled.

"You have a lot of mouth for someone facing jail time," he said.

"First amendment. Read it sometime, fella."

Too much?

"Since you're so keen to talk, how do you answer to these charges?"

"Fifth amendment. Try that, too. I recommend it."

The man closed the folder and stared at her. "This isn't a joke Miss Hines. I know your crowd is all for a good time, but I have the power to make your life very uncomfortable."

She leaned toward him. "Every man has that power, snowflake. Why do you think I'm even here?"

"Ms. Hines, you go too far." His face went red and he stood abruptly. Bertha felt dread run through her. She'd played it all wrong. Should she have been more demure? Have shed a few tears? Men always liked that. She had pushed her luck and now—

Barton sat back down with the cigar he had grabbed from a wooden box and pointed it at her. "Because this is your first offense, and because someone has vouched for you, I'm going to let you go with a warning and a fine. But as for the Cashmere, that's it. I know you think you can do what you want, but we're watching you now. Next time, and there will be a next time if you think you can engage in these immoral acts, I won't be so lenient. No whores, no miscegenation, no funny business. You won't find prison life so amusing by half, I guarantee you that."

He shoved the cigar in his mouth and chomped on it,

staring her down with a look that made her insides quail.

Bertha had no more smart-aleck remarks. She nodded, holding back the anger and frustration that churned in her chest and sought release. Her mind was already clicking ahead, trying to think of how she would get around this. She had to, didn't she? The Cashmere couldn't just close down. She couldn't give up on it that easily.

"You can go," he said.

Barton looked down, dismissing her, and she was escorted out into the main office, drawing leering looks that reminded her she was still dressed for a night in the club. She walked out into the chilly November afternoon and shivered. She'd lost track of time in the jail cell, but the sun would set soon. She had no money for the IRT or trolley, so it would be a long, cold walk back to Harlem.

The honk of a horn from the curb in front of the station got her attention, and she looked over to see Miss Q sitting in the back of a car that had been shined up like a pair of new dance shoes. Her driver got out and opened the door, motioning for Bertha to get in.

She climbed in and accepted the shawl Miss Q handed her. "I take it you were the one who vouched for me?" she asked through chattering teeth.

"An envelope full of cash was all the vouchsafe they needed." She lit one of her cigarettes.

"Why?" Bertha asked as the car pulled into traffic. "Why would you do that for me?"

Unease roiled in her stomach. She owed the woman for real now, and that was no small thing.

Miss Q took a long, slow drag, holding Bertha's gaze as she did. "Why did you teach those classes?" she asked, her words dressed in wisps of smoke. "You expect all those girls to give you something back for the time and money you put into it?"

"No, but—"

"Girl, how do you think I got where I am? I came here from an island no one's even heard of, barely spoke English, and thought I would die in the gutter." Miss Q shook her head. "We help each other. Whenever we can, however we can, using whatever means we got. You got the Cashmere and your knowledge. I got money. If I have to choose between another coat and a sister in need, you best not think you're gonna see me in a new coat come Sunday service."

She took another agitated draw of the cigarette and Bertha felt her throat close up. Not from the smoke, but because Miss Q was right. She thought about the girls trading shifts when one was sick, chipping in to raise money for Cora and her family even though Bertha had already made sure they were comfortable. Women helped each other in ways small and large every day, without thinking, and that was what kept them going even when the world came up with new and exciting ways to crush them.

"Thank you," Bertha said.

Miss Q sucked her teeth in response and looked out the window, but then she nodded her acceptance. "The club was ripped apart. You should know before you get there."

Bertha nodded numbly. "That can be fixed. My girls?"

"Most got away while everything was topsy turvy. Those who were arrested are out now, that I know of."

"And Amir?"

"The cook? Haven't heard anything about him."

"He's not here legally…if they caught him…" Bertha's heart constricted.

Miss Q just looked at her like she was a fool, then shrugged. "If they caught him, they're probably saving you trouble down the line, but I hope for your lovesick self that they didn't."

"And the vote?"

She almost wished she hadn't asked. She couldn't take one more bit of bad news. If the club was ruined and Amir was gone *and* women hadn't won the vote…she just might crack up.

Miss Q exhaled. "Nothing official yet, but it seems like the YES votes are adding up, according to my guys. I don't believe in counting my chicks before they hatch, but we might be at the ballot box next election."

Bertha sagged back against the leather seat and stared out the window, focusing on her relief as the tall buildings and crowded streets of Fifth Avenue passed by. She choked back the emotion blocking her throat and, for just a moment, let herself feel a bit of pure, one hundred fifty proof hope. It was a heady thing.

They would have the vote. Women in New York State would have the vote, and then across the country, because once a change like this started, it wouldn't stop.

The world wouldn't become her oyster overnight. She knew there was still a long road ahead—for women, for Blacks, for Asians, and all those downtrodden people who'd had their rights stripped away while being told they should just be glad they were allowed to call America home. But she knew a thing or two about performing; America had been pulling one over on a good number of its citizens for all these years, and it couldn't do it forever. No one was that good of an actor, not even her. Women winning the vote showed that the Land of the Free had been telling lies since its inception, just as Emancipation had shone light onto truths that many would have preferred stayed hidden. Maybe one day, all the pointless lies would be done with, and everyone could get to that Dream folks liked to talk about so much.

"What're you gonna do now?" Miss Q asked when they pulled up to the Cashmere.

"That depends," Bertha said.

"On a man?" Miss Q asked.

"On *my* man," Bertha said. "On my country."

"And here I thought you was smart." She shook her

head in disappointment, but winked at Bertha as the car pulled away.

Bertha took a deep breath and entered the club. She had to push the door hard because debris was piled up behind it, blocking her path. She took a step inside and all the exhaustion she had been fighting slammed into her. It was destroyed, like a twister had gone through, taking everything of value and making sure it was good and broken. Wall hangings were ripped, chairs and tables in splinters, and glass had been crushed into shards that spread across the floor like sand at Coney Island. She couldn't tell what had been broken when patrons had made a run for it and what the police had gleefully destroyed, but the Cashmere was a shambles.

She clutched her hands to her stomach against the nausea working its way up through her system, trying to fight it down. She'd been building this place up for years, from even before Arthur had passed, giving him ideas and making him think they were his. Slowly crafting it into the place she'd wanted it to become until she'd been in control of it completely. And now it was ruined. She might win the vote once everything shook out, but it seemed she had lost everything else.

Something dropped in the kitchen and she jumped, the echo of the sound through the empty club getting her pulse racing. She started toward the door cautiously; no one knew she had been released, and people might have decided to pick the club over in case she wasn't coming back any time soon. She took up the broken leg of a chair and hefted it in her hand before striding into the kitchen with it raised over her head like one of the batters in the Negro league.

She walked in and found Amir at the stove, humming as he cooked, as though there weren't glass shards at his feet and flour and spices covering the walls. She realized she hadn't expected him to be there. She'd thought that it wasn't possible for her to have the vote and have him, too.

"Amir?"

One second he was stirring and the next he was stalking toward her, pulling her into his arms. He held her tightly and swayed with her, repeating a word over and over until she could make out the sound of it, even if not the meaning.

"Alhamdulilah. Alhamdulilah. You're safe." After that he began murmuring in Bangla, and she only understood the word Allah and her name.

Was he praying for her? She couldn't say the last time she'd appreciated someone doing that, but she let his fervent words wrap around her.

"I saw them take you away," he whispered, his hand sliding up to caress the back of her neck. "And I was so frightened I would never get you back. Anything could have happened to you."

Bertha took a deep breath, and released it.

"Of course nothing happened. I told the coppers I had

something good to come back to," she said, turning to kiss his dimpled cheek.

"The club is wrecked, though," he said, leaning back to look into her face. His expression clouded with regret. "I'm sorry."

She swatted his arm. "I meant you, fool."

She watched as the realization hit him, the smile that stretched across his face, but also the hesitancy in his eyes.

"What is it?" she asked, trying to fight the dread rising to the surface of her skin. Even with his arms around her, she couldn't help but wait for the other shoe to drop.

"I have to make a decision about going home to deal with my land," he said solemnly. His throat worked a moment and his head dipped. "I want you to help me make this decision, but I don't know how to do it without being another man asking you to do something you don't want."

Bertha shucked off the dread like an old snakeskin and lifted her hand to his chest, laying her palm flat.

"The fact that you're even worried about that is a good first step," she said. "Now spill it."

"I did a lot of praying last night, more than I have in a very long time. I couldn't think of what might have been happening to you after seeing the police lead you away. So instead, I asked Allah to keep you safe. And I asked how we could be together. Here."

She couldn't have hidden how his words affected her,

even if she tried.

"And did He have any great insights?" she asked in an unsteady voice, unable to resist teasing him.

He took her hands in his. "Actually…"

epilogue

Five years later

"Okay, catfish curry and fried eggplant, order up!"

Amir glanced over at the plate Cora had made and grinned at her. "Remember all those years ago when you said you weren't sure you'd get the hang of this?"

"I don't know what you're talking about," she said. "I said I wasn't sure I *wanted* to get the hang of this. You're lucky Bertha is a smooth talker."

Amir removed his apron, having handed over the dinner shift to Cora. He could either bound upstairs and shower or spend a bit of time with Bertha before heading out to his meeting; the shower lost by a long shot. "I'm lucky for many things," he said.

"Most especially a friend willing to work in this hot kitchen without complaint?" Syed asked.

"Na, I have no such friends," Amir said, and Syed grinned. "But speaking of luck…"

He headed out of the kitchen and onto the restaurant

floor. He had been worried when he'd proposed his idea to Bertha: the night of the raid, after he'd come down from the apartment and seen the damage, he'd realized she would have to rebuild from scratch. He had some savings, and if he sold his land back home to his cousin or a neighbor, he might have a little more. He'd proposed investing as a partner in her business, handling the restaurant portion while she took care of hosting and entertainment.

She'd been excited, but worried about how to make it work and how to keep her girls safe. He'd given her time to think, but she'd accepted his offer when Janie and Wah Ming had told her they were opening their own private club, run out of an apartment so it drew less scrutiny from the vice squad. They hadn't wanted to disappoint her, but they'd been inspired to strike out on their own. Bertha only had herself to blame for it; the girls—women—had realized they could stand on their own two feet, even if people tried to kick them out from under them.

Building up the business hadn't been easy. Acquiring funds, in addition to Amir's savings and the money from the sale of his land, and Bertha's matching contribution. Coming up with a business plan that suited both of them, which was no easy feat for two stubborn rams. But in the end, 'Bertha's' had finally opened—to little acclaim. But they had worked hard, strategized together, and eventually their sheer will to succeed had bloomed into success. Between the men from the Continent looking for a taste of home, those who had migrated from the South seeking the same, and people just looking to try something different, they were doing quite well. Amir knew that the restaurant business was as temperamental as the sea, but he was just glad he could weather the ups and downs with Bertha at his side.

Amir walked over to the hostess stand after surveying the dining room, not bothering Bertha as she talked to a customer making a reservation. Instead, he peeked down over the side of the wood panels that enclosed the stand.

"Abbu!" Pure happiness filled Amir as his son's eyes grew wide with surprise. Raahil threw his head back and laughed, mouth open wide to reveal the two new teeth that had recently come in. Was that a third, pushing through? His boy was growing up so fast; each new stage of growth pushed Amir to work harder in his fight against injustice. Raahil would soon be old enough to understand the sundry ways his family was seen as less than, and Amir wanted to be sure he never doubted his worth.

"Eh! What's so funny, my shonar chele?"

Done with their customer, Bertha turned around and picked up Raahil, making a silly expression as she pressed her face close to his, which made the boy laugh even more. Then she glanced at Amir, a soft smile still on her face. "We ran out of catfish again. Let's go over sales for the last three weeks tonight and figure out how we need to adjust the next food order. I also need your input on a couple of bands that want to play the Friday night show. And to discuss how to get around these ice distributors bleeding us dry. And…"

Many in the local restaurant group had assumed that having a baby would soften Bertha; after all, wasn't she on her way to becoming "respectable?" He knew they had wished it to be so because she ran circles around the majority of them when it came to business. However, they'd been mistaken; Bertha could now give orders in the same breath as baby talk, and still make sure you knew that the work had better be done fast and to her standards.

"Oh, I love it when you talk figures and food orders," he said, leaning onto the counter and squeezing Raahil's socked foot. "But tonight is the meeting of the Bengali factory workers, love. I'm slated to discuss labor laws and petitioning against the Barred Zone Act."

The right corner of her mouth pulled up.

"And I love it when you talk unionizing and naturalization," she said. He had been joking, but he knew she was not. His heart sped up; she could still do that to him with just a look, even though he had once worried that the sweat and screaming matches of running a business together might tear them apart.

"Will you save me a dance? Later, after Raahil is asleep?"

"I only dance once a month, Amir," she said, then her gaze dropped to his mouth. "But I might be convinced to make an exception."

He wouldn't kiss her in front of the early dinner crowd that had already begun to fill the tables—she was better with public affection than she had been all those years ago, but she still took her roll of boss Bertha very seriously, and so did Amir. Instead, he leaned forward to kiss Raahil's cheek.

"Ami tomake bhalobashi," he whispered in her ear as he pulled away, giving her hand a squeeze.

"I love you, too," she said. She bounced Raahil up and down, but in that moment her gaze was all for him. His Bertha.

Amir walked out into the streets of Harlem. He wasn't sure if he was living the American Dream—things were often hard, and people harder. But the love he had, real, pure, and unshakeable, and the life he had built—they had built—maybe that was better than streets paved with gold. It certainly felt like it to him.

THE END

author's note

Some of the books most helpful in the writing of this novella are as follows:

• *African American Women in the Struggle for the Vote, 1850–1920*, Rosalyn Terborg-Penn. 1998. Bloomington and Indianapolis, Indiana University Press.

• *Bengali Harlem and the Lost Histories of South Asian America*, Vivek Bald. 2013. Cambridge, Massachusetts and London, England, Harvard University Press.

• *Black Women and Politics in New York City*, Julie A Gallagher. 2012. Urbana, Chicago, and Springfield, University of Illinois Press.

• *Sex Workers, Psychics, and Number Runners: Black Women in New York City's Underground Economy*, Lashawn Harris. 2016. Urbana, Chicago, and Springfield, University of Illinois Press.

• *City of Eros: New York City, Prostitution, and the Commercialization of Sex, 1790-1920*, Timothy J. Gilfoyle. 1994. New York City, W. W. Norton & Company.

about the author

Alyssa Cole is a science editor, pop culture nerd, and romance junkie who lives in the Caribbean and occasionally returns to her fast-paced NYC life. When she's not busy writing, traveling, and learning French, she can be found watching anime with her real-life romance hero or tending to her herd of animals.

Find Alyssa at her website, http://alyssacole.com/, on Twitter @AlyssaColeLit and on Facebook at Facebook.com/AlyssaColeLit.